Puppies

Debby Mayne

Published by Forget Me Not Romances, a division of Winged Publications

Copyright © 2018 by Debby Mayne

978-1983704802
ISBN-10: 1983704806

Chapter 1

Never in Emily Moore's life had she ever seen such a sweet face, but she knew she couldn't take on the responsibility of a pet. Or could she?

She'd been out on her own for a while, building a successful business that enabled her to have the house of her dreams. But it was big and lonely, and she often found herself wondering if there was more to life than increasing her bottom line, only to come home to a silent house.

And now here she was, standing in front of Friedman's Shoe Repair Shop, making eye contact with a dog she knew nothing about. She glanced back at the sign in the window with the words *Sweet Great Dane Puppy Free to a Good Home*.

She took a step back and looked the dog in the eyes once again. Her heart jumped smack dab in front of her brain, and she pushed the door open.

The man behind the counter and cobbler, Mr. Friedman, smiled. "Yes? May I help you?"

"I'm interested in the dog." She turned around and pointed to the dog that was now looking over his shoulder at her.

"Are you sure? The puppy is going to be bigger than you when he's full grown." Mr. Friedman gave her a look of amusement.

She blinked. "He's not full grown yet?"

"No." Mr. Friedman came from behind the counter and walked toward the dog. "He's only six months old, so he has quite a bit of growing to do." He pulled a treat out of his pocket. "He's a Great Dane … also known as a gentle giant."

As if to prove the man's point, the dog gently took the treat from the man's hand. Emily's heart melted. Now she knew for sure she wanted him, even though the only dogs she'd ever had were less than half his size.

"What's his name?"

Mr. Friedman grinned. "Hank. I didn't want to name him, but after we found homes for the rest of the litter, the wife said we needed to stop calling him Pup."

Emily nodded. "I like the name Hank." She glanced over at the dog with the tilted head and curious expression that made her laugh. "It suits him."

"Yeah, I thought so too. He's a good dog, but we still have his mama, and our house isn't big enough for two dogs his size." He paused as he looked directly at her. "How would your husband feel about getting a dog that's the size of a horse?"

"I don't have a husband." She looked at Hank, only to have her heart melt even more. "That's why I want Hank. He'll keep me company."

His forehead crinkled. "But I thought you got married last year."

"No, that was my sister Amanda."

He nodded. "Oh, that's right. You're the Moore sister with the big ambitions."

"That's right." Emily forced a smile through gritted teeth. She hated the reputation she'd developed after using her business skills to start businesses, grow them, and sell them for a profit. But she didn't want to ruin her chance of getting this dog that she now knew she had to have.

"Being such a business tycoon, will you have time for Hank? He's a big baby and needs lots of attention."

To prove Mr. Friedman's point, Hank walked over, looked into her eyes again, and lifted a paw. She had to clear her throat to keep her emotions in check.

"He wants you to shake his paw." Mr. Friedman chuckled. "I taught him that trick one afternoon when business was slow."

"So how much do you want for him?" Emily braced herself for a steep dollar amount.

"All I want for him is a good home." He smiled. "But remember he's not cheap. Dogs his size eat like …" He let out a soft chuckle. "They eat like horses."

"You don't want any money?"

"No money. Like I said, just a good home." His attention was diverted to something behind her.

She turned around and saw one of the city councilmen coming toward the shop—a man who'd only been in town a couple of years and decided he wanted to give something back. She'd never spoken to him, but she'd heard good things. As soon as he opened the door, she realized how tall he was—at least a head taller than her five-foot-eight.

He glanced back and forth between Mr. Friedman and Emily before turning back to the shop owner. "I just wanted to check on you to see if you're still entering a float for the children."

"Absolutely. We're doing an *Old Woman and a Shoe* float this year."

"Sounds good." He turned and smiled toward her as he extended his hand. "Hi, I'm Brice Johnson."

"Emily Moore." The instant she took his hand, she felt as though an electric current shot up her arm and straight to her heart.

"Yes, I know. I've heard all about your business acumen."

"Well—"

Mr. Friedman interrupted her. "She doesn't like talking about herself, but we all know that this woman is a business tycoon."

She started to remind him that he couldn't remember which Moore sister she was when she first walked in, but she cleared her throat to stop herself. "I just enjoy starting and growing companies and then handing them over to someone who can enjoy running them."

"Sounds like you live up to your reputation," he said. "How about you? Do you want to be in the parade?"

She scrunched her nose. "No, afraid not. I'm not into that sort of thing."

He tilted his head toward her as a hint of a smile played on his lips. "But you *will* be there, won't you?"

"I'll be standing on the sidewalk watching, if that's what you're asking."

"Good. We need someone to watch." He laughed.

Emily loved the way he laughed so easily and without an ounce of self-consciousness. Hank let out a soft whimper, reminding him he was right there with him.

Brice reached out and scratched Hank behind the ears. "I know one creature who's looking forward to being in the parade."

She tilted her head and gave him a curious look. "Creature?"

Brice nodded. "Yes, Hank's going to be leading the puppy brigade."

"Oh."

Mr. Friedman spoke up. "I was planning to walk him, but if he winds up going home with you, well ..." He held out his hands and exchanged a conspiratorial smile with Brice. "Then he'll be walking with you."

"Oh." She cleared her throat. "I'm not so sure I—"

Brice continued petting Hank. "If you don't want to walk your dog, I'm sure we can find someone who will."

"If you put it that way ..." She glanced down at

Hank before looking back at Mr. Friedman. "You haven't told me I can have the dog yet."

Mr. Friedman grinned. "Well, I could make it conditional that you'll walk him in the parade, but I won't do that to you. All I want for him is a good home where he'll get lots of attention and love."

Brice leaned over and cupped the dog's chin with one hand and rubbed Hank's head with the other, eliciting a goofy expression from Hank. "I have no doubt this guy will do whatever it takes to get all the love he wants."

"Yeah, he pretty much lets you know what he needs and wants." Mr. Friedman turned to Emily with a grin. "I think Hank would love to go home with you."

"So he's mine?"

Mr. Friedman nodded. "Absolutely. And if you still want me to walk him in the parade, I will." Then he scrunched his face, bent over, and rubbed his knee. "That is, if this arthritis doesn't get the best of me."

Guilt instantly washed over her. "You don't have to."

"Someone does." Mr. Friedman held his hand out toward Hank. "He's been looking forward to it ever since he first found out about it."

Emily couldn't help but smile. "I would never want to let him down, so I'll walk with him."

"Oh, good." Brice cleared his throat. "That means you get to join us at the pre-parade meeting and the after-parade party."

"Meeting?" She tilted her head and glanced back and forth between the two men. "Party?"

"I should have said *meetings*," Brice said. "We have several for planning purposes ... you know, to make sure everything runs smoothly."

"Oh, yes, of course."

Mr. Friedman made a grumbling sound. "Meetings are overrated. I don't see why you have to have 'em. Why don't you just tell everyone what to do and let them do it?"

Both Emily and Brice started to talk, so Brice stopped and gestured toward her. "You go first."

She grinned at him. "I agree that there are sometimes too many meetings that go on and on, but a few of them are necessary to make sure everything is coordinated just so."

"That's right," Brice added. "We're only having a few to make sure everyone is clear about what to do, like when to show up, what's expected, and any changes that might take place."

Mr. Friedman looked back and forth between them. "I reckon y'all know what you're talking about, but I still don't like meetings."

"Want to know a secret?" Brice said.

Mr. Friedman narrowed his eyes. "What's that?"

"I don't like meetings either."

"Then why on earth are you on the city council?" Mr. Friedman's voice boomed and echoed through the tiny shop, making Hank's ears twitch. "Sorry, fella. It's just that—"

Brice interrupted. "You really don't like meetings. I get it, which is why I like to keep them short."

"You still didn't answer me about the city

council. Why are you on it?"

With a shrug, Brice replied, "I suppose I like to torture myself … that and the fact that I want to give back to the community that's been so good to me."

Emily listened to this conversation with great interest, but she needed to run a few errands and pick up some things before bringing Hank home with her. So she edged toward the door.

Mr. Friedman lifted and eyebrow. "Leaving without the dog?"

"I just need to pick up some food, a bowl, a leash, a collar, and …" She crinkled her forehead. "What else will I need?"

Both Mr. Friedman and Brice laughed, until Mr. Friedman spoke. "Lots of things for him to chew. He's still a puppy, and unless you want to come home to shredded furniture and shoes with holes, you'll need to get him plenty of things to gnaw on."

"Oh." She hadn't thought about that.

"Having second thoughts?" Mr. Friedman shook his head. "If you've changed your mind about Hank, I certainly understand."

"No, I definitely haven't changed my mind."

Brice lifted his index finger. "Tell you what. If you can wait a few minutes, we can go to the hardware store. We have a pet section that has most of the basics you'll need until you have time to go to a pet store."

"Yeah, he carries premium dog food too." Mr. Friedman folded his arms and shook his head. "Not that most people can afford to feed a dog his size the equivalent of lobster and filet mignon."

Emily could afford to feed him whatever he wanted, but she wasn't about to say that at the risk of sounding arrogant. She'd made enough money in her thirty years to retire in style, but she didn't do it for the money. She loved starting companies and setting people up to live their dreams of working for themselves.

"Why don't you spend a little time here getting to know Hank, while I finish my rounds?" Brice walked toward the door. "I'll come back and get you before I head to the hardware store."

She nodded and then turned around to pet Hank. He looked up at her as if he knew what was going on.

"The two of you really hit it off," Mr. Friedman said.

"I don't see how anyone wouldn't hit it off with Hank. He's such a friendly dog. His expressions are priceless."

"I wasn't talking about the dog." The man smiled. "I was talking about the man."

Chapter 2

Wow. Brice hadn't expected that to happen. As he made his rounds to talk to people about the parade, he couldn't get his mind off Emily. The instant he walked into the shoe shop, he felt as though he'd been smacked right between the eyes.

He knew about the Moore family. Before he joined the city council, he'd been told all about how the town started. Emily's great-great-grandfather had one of the first cars in the county, and as he passed through the area, he thought about what a convenient location for his sales job it was, between two medium sized cities.

So he built a house, brought his family here, and eventually opened a couple of shops to cater to people passing through. Eventually, another family settled in the area, and then another decided to do the same. Within ten years, there was a town that continued to grow as people discovered it.

Now that he'd met Emily, he had no doubt she was cut from the same cloth as her great-great-grandfather. He didn't detect an ounce of indecisiveness or fear in her. She had the same entrepreneurial spirit that it took to start a town. She was smart and nice, and of course, it didn't hurt that she was great to look at.

He didn't spend as much time with each business owner or manager as he'd planned, but that was okay as long as he checked in. Based on personal experience, he knew that his physical presence was important in maintaining a good relationship with the people he counted on. They saw that he cared.

After his final visit, he went back to Mr. Friedman's shop. His heart dropped when he walked in and saw the cobbler alone, standing behind the counter, working on something. Mr. Friedman glanced up and grinned.

"Did they leave already?"

Mr. Friedman chuckled. "You look devastated, so I'm sure you'll be happy to know they just went for a walk around the block. I think Emily wanted a little time alone with Hank."

The first thought that flitted through Brice's mind was that he'd love some time alone with Emily. "So they're coming back?"

"That's the plan ..." Mr. Friedman's grin widened. "Unless they decide to run away." He lifted a handbag from behind the counter. "But I don't think she'd leave this."

A sense of relief washed over Brice. He propped his elbow on the counter, took a brief glance over his shoulder toward the street, and turned back to face Mr. Friedman. "Looks like Emily is smitten."

The cobbler nodded. "Oh, she absolutely is."

"And I'm sure Hank is just as taken by her as she is him."

Mr. Friedman put down the tool he was holding and looked Brice in the eyes. "Hank's not the only one."

Brice gave him a curious look, but before he had a chance to say a word, the sound of the bells on the door caught his attention. The instant he saw that it was Emily returning with Hank, his heart stopped momentarily and then started pounding double-time.

Her slightly windblown hair and flushed cheeks added dimension to her already-breathtaking beauty. And when she smiled at him, the floor beneath him seemed to shift. He leaned into the counter to steady himself.

The sound of Mr. Friedman's voice brought him back to the moment. "How was the walk? Did Hank behave?"

Emily nodded. "Absolutely. Why didn't you tell me he knows everyone in town?"

"I figured you'd find that out soon enough."

"One guy stopped us and asked if Hank was considering a run for mayor." Emily cast a look at Brice and then gave the dog a pat on the head. "Based on how he was today, I think he just might win."

"I'm sure everyone in town would be thrilled to have him sitting in the mayor's chair," Brice added.

Emily gave him an apologetic look. "I didn't mean—"

"No, I realize you were just kidding. Hank's a lovable fella."

"I know, right?" Emily shifted from one foot to the other, and Hank adjusted his body to lean into her. "When will you be ready to take me to get some stuff for him?"

"We can do it now."

Emily turned to Mr. Friedman. "Do you mind if I leave him here while we do this?"

"You can bring him with us," Brice said.

Mr. Friedman shook his head. "Why don't the two of you go without him? I'd love to watch him for a few minutes." He came around from behind the counter and placed his hand on Hank's shoulder. "I'd like some time to say goodbye to the big guy, if you don't mind."

As Brice led Emily from the store, he looked over his shoulder to see Mr. Friedman give him a thumbs-up. It was obvious that the man had more than one motive to keep the dog with him a few more minutes ... and Brice appreciated it.

"Mr. Friedman is giving me the leash and collar. What else do I need besides food, bowls, and chew toys?"

"Have you thought about something for him to sleep on?" Brice paused. "We have an extra large dog bed that's been sitting on the shelf for almost a year. I need to make space for something that'll actually sell, so I can give that to you."

She shook her head. "I don't want you to give it to me. I can buy it."

"I was going to put it on clearance anyway, so you'll get a good deal on it." He tilted his head and met her gaze. "You will take a good deal, won't you?"

"Of course. I'm a bargain hunter at the core."

That simple statement made him like her even more. "Since he's still a puppy, he'll continue to grow for a while. The bed is extra large, but he might wind up hanging off the edge."

She shrugged. "Then I'll just have to make one if and when that happens."

"Make one?" He studied her face.

"Yes. I can sew. In fact, that's one of the first businesses I started."

"Sewing? You were a seamstress?"

She shook her head. "No, I took a tailoring class. Do you know William Evans?"

"Absolutely. He has Mooreville Tailoring." Brice paused as he thought about the last job he brought to William. "He's the best tailor I think I've ever had."

Emily grinned. "I know. He was the best tailor I had working for me, so that's why I offered him the business when I was ready to sell it."

Brice chuckled. "Is there anything you can't do?"

"Of course." She cleared her throat. "But if it's something I want to know how to do, I find a way to learn it."

"You're pretty special."

"I don't know about special, but I am curious

and enjoy learning new things."

This woman intrigued Brice. He'd never met anyone like her, and nothing would make him happier than getting to know her better.

When they arrived at the hardware store, she took a long look around. "You've changed things around."

"I wanted to add a few items, and this seemed the most efficient way to do it." He gestured toward the closest aisle. "This is where I have all the seasonal merchandise."

"Most people have seasonal in the back of the store so customers will have to walk past other merchandise to get to it."

"I tried that, but a lot of folks didn't know it was here, so I moved it front and center. Sales went up significantly after I did this."

"Where's the pet section?"

He pointed to the back of the store. "Until I figure out a better place, I have it over there."

Without waiting for him to take the lead, she took off toward the direction of the pet aisle. He had to walk fast to keep up with her.

"Wow. You weren't kidding when you said you had everything I'd need to get started." She took a long look around. "Who needs a pet store when they can come here and get anything they want."

"Not everything." The moment she looked at him, he felt that shifting sensation once again. He turned toward the pet food to keep from losing his focus. "We only have a few selections of food. Pet stores have every kind you can imagine. And I only have three sizes of water and food bowls."

"Okay, I get the point." She picked up the biggest bowl on the shelf. "I'll obviously need this." She paused and glanced around. "I'm thinking I might need a basket."

"I'll go get you one."

As Brice headed toward the front of the store, he realized he should have grabbed a basket on the way in. But he was so mesmerized by Emily, everything but her was a blur.

By the time he returned, she had quite a load lined up on the floor. She gave him an embarrassed look. "I don't know what chew toys he'll prefer, so I'm getting these …" She gestured toward her pile of dog toys. "What do you think?"

"Well, based on my experience with what most people with big puppies buy, I'd probably stick to a couple of things, like this." He reached over and picked up a big, squeaky hamburger. "And this." With the other hand, he grabbed a bag of extra large rawhides."

"That's all?"

"I think so, at least in the beginning. Too many new toys might confuse him. If you give him one new toy at a time, along with the rawhide, he'll be able to enjoy it more."

"That's what I hear parents say about their kids." She walked around her large selection of dog toys before bending over and putting them back on the shelf. "What else do I need?"

"Don't forget about the bed … unless you want him sleeping in bed with you." He grinned at her.

"No, that's okay. Where are the beds?"

He took her to the end of the aisle, where he had the pet beds stacked high. "I'll have to get a ladder to get the biggest one off the top. I hope you're okay with the red and blue plaid."

"Plaid, huh?" She tapped her index finger on her chin. "That'll be fine."

"Wait right here."

As Brice got the ladder, rolled it over to the dog bed shelf, and climbed to the top, he was aware of Emily carefully watching him. He had to take a few deep breaths and force himself to focus on his task, rather than let his feelings for her throw him off balance.

When he placed the bed at her feet, she looked down at it and then up at him. "So you're saying this won't work when he's full grown? It looks pretty big to me."

"It might still work, but he's going to be quite a bit bigger than he is now." He pushed the ladder away to give them more room on the aisle. "Are you starting to have second thoughts?"

"Absolutely not. I already love Hank."

"I get it." The image of Emily walking Hank flitted through his mind. "One look at those big, soulful eyes, and he has anyone wrapped around his …" Brice laughed at himself. "I started to say little finger, but he doesn't have fingers."

"Then I suppose I'm wrapped around his toe." She joined him in laughter.

Brice saw something coming toward them out of the corner of his eye. "Watch out."

Chapter 3

The second Emily looked up and saw Hank coming toward her with determination she took a step back and stumbled. Fortunately, Brice was right behind her to keep her from falling into the shelves.

Hank glanced down at the bed on the floor and appeared to try to stop, but he slid about a foot and wound up falling onto it. Emily bent over to make sure he was okay, but when he looked into her eyes as he lay on the bed, she saw that he was just fine. He even seemed happy if the look on his face was any indication.

"I think he likes his bed," Emily said.

"I'm sure he likes it much better than the old army blanket he's been sleeping on. He'll think he hit the jackpot at your house." Mr. Friedman had come in with Hank, but until now, his presence wasn't even noticed. "Right, Hank?" He bent over and rubbed behind the dog's ears, eliciting a sigh from the humongous puppy.

Emily saw that Hank already took up the majority of the bed. "You're right about needing something large. If he grows much bigger, he'll need a new bed."

"Now we need to pick some food." Brice gestured toward the selection. "We're somewhat limited, but I'm sure something here will suffice until you get to the pet store."

Mr. Friedman pointed to one of the bags of puppy food. "That's what I've been feeding him, and he seems to like it."

"I suppose I should get the biggest bag you have."

The older man nodded. "You got that right. He's a big eater, but that will decrease over time. I hope you're getting the biggest bowl here."

"She is." Brice picked it up and stuck it in the basket. "I'll give you a discount."

"I'm not asking for—"

Mr. Friedman interrupted her. "You don't have to ask. He gives all his important customers a discount. Just take it."

One of the reasons Emily was so driven was her pride. In spite of the fact that her ancestors founded the town, her parents didn't have much. People assumed they were well to do.

"I'll even deliver everything to your house," Brice said, snapping her out of her thoughts.

"That's sweet of you, but I don't want you going to all that trouble." She cleared her throat.

"I'm not really getting all that much, so I should be able to handle it."

"I need to run a few errands anyway, so it's no trouble." The finality of the tone of his voice let her know he wasn't open for arguing.

"Okay, thank you."

Mr. Friedman handed her the leash he'd taken off Hank. "You'll need to put this on him before you leave the store. Hank is a friendly dog, and if he sees someone he knows, he'll take off after them."

Brice nodded. "And he's not kidding. I've chased that dog more times than I can count."

"I suppose I need to enroll him in some obedience training."

"Not a bad idea," Brice agreed. "They offer several at the Pampered Pet."

Mr. Friedman grinned and tilted his head toward her. "Having second thoughts yet? It's not too late to change your mind."

"No, not at all. In fact, it'll be nice to have something besides work to do with my time."

"I agree." Mr. Friedman took a step back. "Don't hesitate to call if you need me. I have my shop phone calls forwarded to my cell phone at night."

"Thanks. I'll stop by tomorrow and let you know how things go."

After he left, Brice gathered everything, put it into the cart, and started toward the front of the store. Once they reached the checkout, he placed everything on the counter. "She gets the Valued Customer discount."

The cashier nodded and began ringing

everything up. It only took her a couple of minutes, and as she finished scanning each item, Brice placed it back in the basket. Emily just stood there watching and holding Hank's leash.

Once everything was back in the cart and paid for, he gestured toward the door. "I can follow you home with all this."

As difficult as it was for Emily to accept help, she nodded and headed toward her SUV. "C'mon, Hank. Let's go home."

He hopped right up onto the backseat and sat there like a little man. She couldn't help but laugh at the comical expression on his face.

Every now and then, she glanced in the rearview mirror and saw Hank's face as he looked out the side window. Never once did he try to get in the front seat with her. In fact, he was extremely well behaved, until they pulled up in front of the house she'd purchased last year, after making her biggest sale ever.

The instant she turned off the ignition, Hank started jumping around and letting out a few soft, "Woof," sounds.

She laughed again as she got out and opened the back door. "I can tell life will never be dull with you in my life."

He tilted his head and gave her a curious look as she took hold of the leash. He got out and kept pace with her all the way up to the front door.

By the time she had the door unlocked, Brice was on the porch with all of Hank's new things. "Nice place you have here." He put down the bag of food and gave the dog a pat on the head. "You're a fortunate dog to live in such a great house with such a nice lady, Hank."

"I'm the fortunate one."

Brice straightened up and looked her in the eyes. "This is a nice house."

"Thank you." Emily had to fight the urge to explain how hard she'd worked to get it. Based on prior experiences with anyone she'd tried to explain her life to, it would be futile. People either didn't believe her, or they acted like they thought someone had given her a break.

"You did this all on your own, didn't you?"

Maybe he did understand. She nodded. "Pretty much."

"I'm impressed. I don't know many people our age who would have been able to accomplish what you have."

"Look at you."

He gave her a questioning look. "What do you mean by that?"

"You own a business, and you're on the city council."

He smiled. "Yes, I own a business, but it was already up and running when I bought it with the money I got from a corporate buyout of my contract. That was much easier than what you've done."

"I'm not so sure." She decided it was time to change the subject. "Come on in while I get Hank's things set up."

At first, he looked like he might accept her invitation, but he slowly shook his head. "I need to go back to the store and get it ready for the big sale we're starting tomorrow."

She didn't know much about matters of the heart like she was facing now, but taking care of business was one thing she completely understood. "Maybe some other time then."

"Yes," he said with a smile. "I'll take you up on that."

After he left, she turned to Hank and smiled. He'd remained sitting on the floor beside her, watching the back and forth conversation as though he understood everything they said.

"Are you thirsty? Let's get you some water." She picked up the bowl, washed it out, filled it with water, and set it on the floor.

He walked over to it and started drinking … and drinking and drinking until the bowl was completely dry. So she picked it up and filled it again. Apparently, he'd had as much water as he wanted because he didn't even bother walking over to the bowl.

Over the next few minutes, Emily arranged all the new dog items she'd purchased. She put some food in the bowl and placed it beside the water. He had a few nibbles and took a break to follow her around the house. When she placed the dog bed beside her own, he looked up at her with that soulful expression that had grabbed her heart when they first met.

"You are an interesting dog, Hank."

He tilted his head and let out another, "Woof."

"Want to go outside?"

His ears twitched as he glanced at the window. Apparently, he understood the meaning of the word *outside*.

"Good thing this house had a fence when I bought it," she said as they walked toward the back door. "I never would have thought to put one up."

She opened the door, but he just stood there looking at her. So she stepped outside, and he followed.

As Hank walked around the backyard and sniffed everything, including every bush and flower, she stood and watched. There was definitely something special about this dog, and she didn't have an ounce of remorse about getting him.

He took his time getting familiar with the yard, so she continued standing there, thinking about everything that had transpired in such a short time. That morning when she left the house, she had no idea she'd come home with a dog she adored and have thoughts of a man who'd wormed his way into her mind and wouldn't leave.

Hank turned around and met her gaze. "Woof."

"I'm still right here," she said with a chuckle.

After he finished checking out the yard, he joined her by the door. Before she had a chance to say another word, her phone rang.

It was Mr. Friedman. "How are you and Hank getting along?"

"So far, so good."

"Just making sure. I want you and Hank to be happy."

She looked at Hank who stood facing the door as if waiting for it to open so he could go inside. "I'm happy, and I'm pretty sure Hank is too. He's staying close to me, everywhere I go."

"That's Hank for ya." Mr. Friedman chuckled. "He was like that with my wife too. I reckon we can call him a lady's man."

"I'll probably take him around with me most days."

"Not a bad idea. He loves being out and about—such a social creature. And he knows most of the people downtown. He's up to date on his shots, but you'll need to take him in for some boosters in a few months. Stop by the shop sometime tomorrow, and I'll give you the information and paperwork you'll need."

After she got off the phone, she brought Hank inside and watched him finish eating the bowl of food. He was so entertaining to watch she realized she hadn't even thought about her favorite TV show or the book she'd been reading.

"Want to go for a walk?"

Once again, his ears twitched with understanding. He stood very still as she attached the leash to his collar, and then he led the way to the front door.

It was nearly dark out now, but the streetlights provided enough light to see where they were going. A couple of her neighbors were out walking their dogs. She tensed, as one of them got close. This was the first time she'd even thought about how Hank might be with other dogs.

To her relief, he walked up to the dog that was about a third his size and wagged his tail. Her neighbor, on the other hand, looked terrified.

Chapter 4

Brice arrived at the store the next morning before the sun came up. He'd done most of the preparation for the sale last night, but there were still a few things that needed tending to before he unlocked the doors to the public.

He put some of the change in the cash drawer and the rest of it in the vault behind his office. When he came out, he spotted someone standing outside the door. He flipped the light switch and saw that it was Emily and Hank, so he opened the door.

"What happened?"

"Nothing." Emily made a funny face as she gestured toward Hank. "He woke me up at the crack of dawn, so I took him for a walk. He led me here."

Brice had to stifle a laugh. "You're the one who should lead the dog. You definitely need to take him to obedience training."

"I know." She remained standing there as if she didn't know what to do. He suspected that was a different kind of experience for her.

"Would y'all like to come in while I get the place ready? We're having our first sale of the season starting today."

"I don't want to bother you."

Too late for that. Merely the sight of her bothered him—in a good way. "You're fine. I have some coffee brewing in the break room, but maybe you can give me a hand with something first."

"Sure." She followed him toward the garden center. "I need to unwrap the cord around these pallets so the garden people can pull things out as the floor stock gets picked over."

Hank plopped down as if he knew he'd have to wait. Brice smiled. "Smart dog."

"I'm starting to wonder if he might be too smart for me."

"I don't think so. You just need some time to figure him out, and if you take him to training, it won't be long before he knows who's in charge."

She smiled. "What I'd like to start with is the first-thing-in-the-morning thing. I'm an early riser, but Hank has me beat."

Brice tried to put on a sympathetic face. "I'm sure y'all will work that out over time." He walked around to the other side of the pallet. "Would you mind giving me a hand with this rope?"

"Of course I don't mind."

Over the next fifteen minutes, they unwrapped that pallet and prepped a few other areas of the store. Once they were done, Brice brushed his hands.

"That would have taken me more than twice as long if I had to do it alone. Let's get some coffee."

On the way to the break room, Brice grabbed a bowl from the pet section. Once they got to the small area in the back, he filled the bowl with water from the small sink and placed it on the floor for Hank.

He pulled a couple of mugs from the cabinet above the coffee pot and looked over his shoulder at Emily. "How do you like your coffee?"

"A whisper of cream."

He laughed. "I've never heard it put like that before. I'll try to get it right and not give you a shout of cream."

Once he had two mugs filled with coffee—one with what he hoped was the right amount of whisper and the other one straight up black—he sat down at the table with Emily. She accepted her mug, took a sip, and nodded. "Just right."

The coffee wasn't the only thing that was just right. As he sat across the table from her, he realized that he was intrigued by everything about Emily Moore, from the slight upward curve of the corners of her lips to her athletic build. Even her hair that had a slight windblown look took his breath away.

"Hank is something else." The soft tone of her voice made him smile.

"Something else in a good way, or—"

"Definitely in a good way." She laughed. "Who needs entertainment when he's around? I can sit and watch him all evening without getting bored."

"I'm surprised you have time for any entertainment at all." He stopped himself before he added he didn't see how she'd have time for Hank who obviously needed a tremendous amount of attention.

"I'm not an all-work kind of girl." She took a sip of her coffee and placed the mug on the table. "At least I don't want to be. Unfortunately, there have been times when I've neglected everything but work."

"Trust me, I understand." He paused and offered her what he hoped was an understanding smile.

"I know you do. Only a business owner would understand."

That simple statement said a lot, and it made him feel better than anything else she could have said. It was nice to know she believed him. "I've been guilty of burning the midnight oil with my business."

"It's hard not to do that, with everything a business needs ... and there's always something that needs to be done."

"If you want to tell me this is none of my business, that's fine, but I'm wondering why you decided to get a dog."

She let out a chuckle. "I'm wondering the same thing. But after we settled in last night, I realized I've been missing something important, and it was really nice to have him right there beside me."

"Maybe I should get a dog."

She lifted one eyebrow in a comical manner as

a hint of a smile played on her lips. "Maybe you should."

"I can even bring a dog to work with me since I own the place."

She nodded. "True."

His gaze locked with hers, and he felt as though the floor fell out from beneath him. That same feeling he couldn't describe that happened to him every single time they looked at each other. And instead of decreasing in intensity, it increased exponentially.

"Or if you want, you can borrow Hank to hang out here ... at least until you find your perfect dog match."

Laughter escaped Brice's throat. "Do you think you can spare him, even for a little while?"

"He hasn't even been with me a whole day," she replied. "But I have to admit he's gotten under my skin."

Hank's ears twitched as he sat beside them, looking back and forth as they spoke. There was no doubt in Brice's mind that he knew they were talking about him, and he seemed to love it.

Brice patted Hank on the head. "For a puppy, you sure are smart."

"I think it's more of a sense thing than smarts," Emily admitted.

Brice leaned back and studied the woman and her dog. He'd known about Emily ever since he'd moved to Mooreville, and he'd seen her around town. But until yesterday, he didn't fully grasp all the great things he'd heard about her. One of his pals said she was the smartest person in town, but

Brice assumed that was based on her obvious business acumen. Another guy said she was elusive to the point of being an ice queen, and she shot guys down so fast no one dared ask her out. She definitely wasn't an ice queen from what Brice had seen.

"So what are your plans for the day?" He leaned back in the small chair and smiled at her.

"I'd planned to do some research on a new business, but I might wait until tomorrow for that." She glanced over at Hank. "I'm thinking it might be better to spend some time with my new buddy."

"You don't take much time off, do you?"

She shook her head. "No, and that's one of the reasons I decided Hank was just what I needed." She paused. "When it's just me, there doesn't seem to be a reason to take time off."

"I get that." Brice had spent quite a few nights in his hardware store thinking of ways to increase his bottom line. "But I've discovered that a little down time can actually increase productivity."

"I've heard that." She gave him a sheepish look. "Unfortunately, I never even considered putting it into practice."

"Same here." Brice stared at his coffee mug for a few seconds before an idea struck him. "Why don't we have a little down time together?"

"Sure. When?"

"Today."

She narrowed her eyes and stared at him. "I thought you had a sale going on today."

"I do, but I also have some extremely capable staff who can run this place without me." He

31

cleared his throat. "I think it's time I let them do it too."

"Okay, so what do you want to do?"

He gave her a half smile. "I was hoping you'd think of something."

She laughed. "We're a mess, aren't we? I mean, after all, here we are, two adults who own and run businesses, and we don't even know what to do when we're not working."

"Why don't we leave here—as soon as my employees arrive, that is—and go figure it out?"

"Sounds good to me."

He stood up. "Want more coffee?"

She started to shake her head, but she stopped and nodded. "Sure, that sounds good."

As they sipped their next cup of coffee together, Hank alternated between sitting and lying down. Never once did he seem anxious or eager to leave.

Brice finished the last sip of coffee and stood to carry his mug to the sink before turning around to face Emily. "We could take a lesson from him."

"I'm sure there are a lot of lessons we could learn from him, but what, specifically, are you talking about?"

"He knows how to relax and take things as they come."

She looked at her dog and nodded. "Yeah, he's pretty good at that."

After Emily finished her coffee, he cleaned her mug and picked up the leash. "So Hank, my man, what do you want to do today?"

Hank scrambled to his feet and let out a soft,

"Woof."

"I sure wish I understood what he was saying."

Brice held out his hands. "I'm not one hundred percent positive, but I think he said he'd like to go to the dog park."

Emily imitated Brice's gesture. "I should have figured that out for myself. When will your employees get here?"

As if on cue, a couple of people wearing the store polo shirts walked into the break room to put their lunches in the refrigerator. Brice explained what was going on and said if they needed him, he'd have his phone ringer on.

Ross gave him a thumbs-up. "We've got this, boss."

"Everything in the garden center is twenty percent off, except the perennials. They're thirty percent off."

Melba and Ross exchanged a knowing look. "Yes, we're aware of that. And all the winter merchandise is half off." She tilted her head toward Brice. "You two go on and have some fun. Don't worry about us. We've both been here long enough to know what to do."

"I know you do." Brice gestured toward the door. "After you, Emily and Hank."

They hadn't gotten out the door when Brice overheard Melba say, "It's about time he did something besides work."

"I think he was just waiting for a pretty girl to come along."

Brice turned to Emily to see if she might have heard. If her flaming red cheeks were any indication, she heard every word.

The three of them walked half a block before he finally took Emily's hand. He wasn't sure she'd be okay with that, but the only way he'd know was to try.

Chapter 5

Emily hadn't experienced this giddy sensation of puppy love since early high school. After that little romance fizzled shortly after it began, she decided falling for a guy wasn't worth the heartache. She'd fallen into a pattern of focusing on everything but matters of the heart and hadn't bothered to break it.

"Whatcha thinking?" Brice asked as they turned the corner toward the dog park.

"Just silly thoughts." She wasn't about to tell him what was really on her mind. "I wonder if Hank has ever been to the dog park."

Brice leaned down and looked Hank in the eyes. "How about it? Have you ever been to the dog park?"

Hank's ears twitched, and then he picked up his pace. Both Brice and Emily laughed.

As they made the last turn toward the park, Emily noticed that Hank had started panting. "I think he's been there, and he's excited about going back."

"No kidding. Mr. Friedman must have taken him there in the past."

The instant they arrived at the park gate, Hank turned and looked Emily in the eyes. "Want me to let you loose?"

He let out another, "Woof."

Emily's ancestors were animal lovers, so they put a tremendous amount of their attention on making sure the citizens had plenty of ways to enjoy their pets. This dog park was the result of a bequest by one of her great-great uncles who had a menagerie of dogs, cats, birds, and various reptiles in his mansion on the edge of town.

A chest-high chain link fence enclosed an area the size of an average city block. It featured a variety of equipment to provide exercise and entertainment for dogs as well as plenty of benches for their people. There were also plenty of pet waste stations scattered around, along with signs for owners to pick up after their four-legged friends.

Emily studied Brice's expressions as he looked around the park. "Have you ever been here before?"

He shook his head. "No. Until now, I never had a reason to." He smiled down at her. "How about you?"

She nodded. "I used to come with my grandfather."

"What kind of dog did he have?"

"He had several as I was growing up. My

favorites were the German Shepherd and Yorkie. They were the best of friends, in spite of the difference in their sizes." She explained how much her family had always loved animals and that she was the only Moore she knew of who waited so long to have a pet.

"I wonder where he came up with the concept for this place."

"My great-great-uncle saw a dog park in one of the bigger cities, and he thought it was a great idea since so many people chose to live in town rather than out in the country." She gestured around. "So he took everything he liked and added a few more things to bring it here to Mooreville."

"I'm impressed." Brice shifted to face Emily. "I remember the first time I saw this in the city budget and thought it was odd that there would be one line item that didn't have to be covered by taxes."

She smiled at him. "Based on what my family has told me, the cost of running this place is covered for the next several generations."

"It is."

"Does it bother you?"

He narrowed his eyes and gave her a curious look. "No, not at all. Why do you ask?"

She shrugged. "There have been a few people in town who think the money could be put to better use. In fact, one entire family—aunts, uncles, cousins, and all—left Mooreville over this park. They wanted to have a nicer community center and thought that the funds should be reallocated."

"That wouldn't be right. The person who left the money for this dog park should have his wishes honored. It's not like the tax payers are out that money."

Emily appreciated his insight. "Absolutely."

"Well, now that we have that settled, let's see what Hank's up to." Brice stood and extended his hand to help her up.

Hank had found a friend—a bulldog puppy that appeared in awe of the big dog. They ran around in circles, taking turns leading.

Emily laughed as she shook her head. "I don't think Hank realizes how big and goofy he looks."

"He's clearly having a blast with that little pooch." Brice paused to watch the dogs a few more seconds. "I wonder what the bulldog thinks."

The sound of someone approaching from the side caught their attention. "My little guy is having the time of his life with your dog."

Emily spun around and found herself face-to-face with someone who appeared to be about her age, but she'd never seen her before. She extended a hand. "Hi, I'm Emily Moore."

The woman shook Emily's hand. "I'm Charlotte Ramsey, and my dog is Biscuit." She turned to Brice. "Are you Mr. Moore?"

Brice cleared his throat. "No, I'm Brice Johnson."

Charlotte's face turned red as she lifted her fingertips to her lips. "Oh, sorry. I just assumed …" Her voice trailed off as she glanced away.

"Don't worry about it," Brice said. "I don't think I've seen you around before. Are you new in town?"

Charlotte nodded. "I just got transferred here

by the Recreational Facilities Corporation."

"Oh." Brice nodded his understanding. "You're the new manager for the skating rink."

"Yes, that would be me."

"They said they were bringing in someone who could turn the place around."

Charlotte gave Brice a confused look. "How do you know this?"

Now Emily felt as though she needed to speak up. "Brice is on the city council, and he knows stuff like that before everyone else in town finds out."

Charlotte nodded. "That makes sense. They've had a lot of trouble with the rink here, and they thought I might be able to do something about it."

Emily was aware of the problems since many of them included crimes that made it to the front page of the *Mooreville Gazette*. "I used to go to the skating rink when I was a teenager. That was before all the problems."

"And that's what my goal is—to bring it back to pre-problem days. I want parents to feel good about dropping their teens and preteens off without worrying about their kids getting in trouble with the law."

"If there's anything I can do, let me know." Emily stuck her hand in her pocket and pulled out a card. "Here's my number where I can be reached almost any time."

"I'll be glad to do what I can too," Brice added. "I don't have the same skills Emily has, but if you tell me what you need, I follow directions well."

Charlotte glanced back and forth between Emily and Brice and then nodded. "Thanks, y'all. I suppose I don't have to tell you that the place was a wreck when I started working there."

Emily shook her head. "Last time I went to the skating rink was when it was for sale. It was pretty much abandoned."

"I can't say I blame the parents for not wanting to take their kids skating," Charlotte admitted. "But we've already gutted the interior, and I have a team of painters coming to freshen up the outside."

Brice nodded. "The city is looking at the permits for all the work. Looks like you're doing everything you can to bring it up to code."

"I've done this before, but this one is the biggest challenge. I understand the city recreation department does such a good job it's hard to compete with them."

"Why would you want to compete with them?" Emily asked. "Maybe you should talk to the director about running some programs together."

"What a great idea." A humongous grin spread across Charlotte's face. "I'll call first thing in the morning and see if I can get a meeting." She paused momentarily. "I know the recreation director's first name is Noah ..."

Emily nodded. "And his last name is Chambers. He's a good guy, and I'm sure he'll be happy to work with you. He's done a few joint ventures before, so he knows what is and isn't allowed by the city."

"Thank you so much." Charlotte's dog came running toward them, and she knelt down. "Having fun with your new friend?"

Biscuit wagged his nubby little tail so hard his

whole body wiggled. Hank approached on Charlotte's other side and melted into her when she gave him a rub between the ears.

Emily chuckled. "Hank likes you."

Charlotte smiled up at her. "From what I can see, Hank likes pretty much everyone and everything."

Hank leaned harder into Charlotte and looked up at her with his expressive eyes. Everyone laughed. Emily didn't think her heart could melt any more, but it did.

"I've always heard that Great Danes were sweet dogs," Charlotte said. "And now I know it's true. How long have you had him?"

"I just got him yesterday."

Brice spoke up. "She got him from Mr. Friedman, over at the shoe repair shop."

A look of dawning came over Charlotte. "I thought I'd seen him before. Mrs. Friedman was leaving the shop with him as I was going in with my boots."

Hank let out another, "Woof," making everyone laugh again.

"I'm pretty sure he knows we're talking about him," Emily said.

Charlotte nodded. "Oh, I'm sure he does. Biscuit gets excited when I talk about him too."

Biscuit chose that moment to put his front paws up on Charlotte's leg, his tail still wagging so fast it was a blur. Emily sighed. She never imagined enjoying something so simple ... so basic as hanging out at the dog park, talking about her pet.

"I need to run." Charlotte took a step toward

the gate before stopping momentarily. "I have to get Biscuit home and meet some contractors who think they can repair the floors, although I'm rather doubtful."

"You'll be surprised at what flooring people can do," Brice said.

"I sure hope so. Replacing all the wood in the rink is quite pricy."

After Charlotte left, Brice turned to Emily. "I think the two of you can be good friends. She seems smart, nice, and ambitious, just like you."

"Thanks for the smart and nice comment, but …" She wasn't sure how she felt about being called ambitions.

"When I said ambitious, I meant that in a good way."

"Okay, then, thank you for that too. I just don't want anyone to think I'm the kind of person who'll stop at nothing to make a business deal."

Brice glanced down at the ground and then looked up at her. "Do you want to do something later?"

She was fully aware that he didn't comment on what she'd said, which was fine, except now she'd wonder if there was a reason. "Like what?"

He shrugged. "Like maybe dinner?"

Her first inclination was to turn him down, but she stopped herself and decided to let go a little bit more. "Okay. What did you have in mind?"

"We could stay in town and go to the Mooreville Diner, or maybe we can go into Raleigh."

One of her cousins owned the Mooreville

Diner. "Let's find someplace in Raleigh."

"Sounds good to me."

Hank was still running around the park, but he didn't appear to be having as much fun as when Biscuit was there. All she had to do was hold up the leash and say his name for him to come running toward them.

"If I'd known having a dog was this easy, I would have done it a long time ago."

Brice made a goofy face. "You've only had him for a day. I don't think it's always this easy."

Hank let out another, "Woof."

Chapter 6

After they walked back to the hardware store, Emily took Hank home. Brice couldn't keep his mind off Emily, so finally Melba told him he was in the way. "Why don't you go on home and plan your next date with the pretty girl?"

He hesitated. "I don't know."

Ross waved his hand toward the door. "We've got this. It's not like it's the first time we've worked a sale."

Melba came around from behind the counter, placed her hand on his shoulder, and nudged him toward the exit. "Trust me, Brice. We'll be just fine." She grinned as they made eye contact. "Besides, we know how to get in touch with you if necessary."

"And unless the place burns down, it won't be necessary."

Brice shook his head. "If the place burns down, don't call me. Call the fire department."

"You got it, boss." Melba did a mock salute. "Now go on. Get outta here."

"Yes, ma'am." He returned the salute.

All the way home, he ran different ideas of things to do through his head. He could clean the place, but that was too much like work. Besides, his place didn't get that messy since he was rarely home.

Another thought was to sit down and read one of the trade magazines he had stacked in his room. But that was still work related.

Brice couldn't help but laugh at himself. Throughout high school and college, he found every way possible to get out of hard work. And now all he knew how to do was work. It was like someone had flipped a switch and turned him into a robot that didn't know anything else.

As soon as he walked into the house he'd lived in since moving to Mooreville, he decided to go to the gym for a quick workout. He'd joined nearly a year ago, but after the first couple of months, he hadn't found the time to go. He made a mental note to change that.

The workout lasted a little more than an hour. When he got home, he prepared a late lunch and sat down in front of the TV. Unfortunately, nothing held his attention, so he turned off the TV, picked up his plate, and headed for the kitchen table, grabbing one of the trade magazines on the way.

He tried to concentrate on the article about some of the newer tools using modern technology, but Emily's image popped into his mind over and over. Finally, he took the last bite of his sandwich, closed the magazine, and went to the bathroom to take a shower. It was early, but he wouldn't get too dirty between now and when it was time to pick her up for their dinner date.

As soon as he stepped out of the shower, he heard his cell phone ring. He quickly wrapped a towel around his waist and went to the chest of drawers where he'd put his cell phone. It was Emily.

"Is everything okay?"

She cleared her throat. "Everything's fine, except I don't know what to do with myself, so I called your store. They said you left for the day. I know I probably shouldn't do this, but I wondered if you might be interested in getting together a little earlier."

He couldn't help but smile. "There's nothing wrong with your calling me. In fact, I'm going through the same thing. Face it, Emily. We're just a couple of workaholics who don't know how to take time off to relax."

"I know, right?"

"So what do you have in mind?"

"In mind?"

"Did you forget that you called me to see if I wanted to get together early?"

She let out a giggle. "Oh yeah, that's right." She paused. "Let's see. We can go for another walk or maybe do a little window shopping or—"

"Why don't we just park somewhere in Raleigh and head wherever we feel like going?"

"Sounds good."

After he hung up, he whistled as he finished getting ready. Then he stopped and faced himself in the mirror. He looked different. And now that he thought about it, he felt different. More relaxed. Less focused on how to improve the bottom line.

And he liked it.

What made him feel even better was the fact that he wasn't in this alone. He got to share the experience of backing off of work and enjoying leisure time with one of the prettiest, smartest, and most understanding women he'd ever known. Most of the women he'd dated had a difficult time understanding why his business was so important, but they didn't seem to mind the fact that he was financially successful, regardless of their station in life. Emily not only understood, she was the female version of him.

He'd always heard that opposites attracted, but his relationship with Emily so far was proving something completely different. The biggest part of their attraction was the fact that they were similar and understood what made the other one tick.

He wasn't sure what to wear, so he stood in his closet for a while staring at the pitifully sad selection. It wasn't that he didn't have the means to get new clothes. It was more that he didn't have the time to shop or a good enough reason to get something new. Maybe that would change, now that he'd finally met someone.

After pulling out a few things, he finally settled on some casual slacks that weren't jeans and a long-sleeve button-front shirt. It was still cool at night, so he grabbed one of his V-neck pullovers from the side of his closet that he rarely touched.

He pulled up in front of her house, hesitated only for a few seconds before getting out of his truck, and walked up to her front door. He didn't have a chance to ring her doorbell before she flung it open. Standing right next to Emily was Hank who tilted his head and let out his familiar, "Woof."

Emily flashed her stunning smile as she stepped aside to let him in. "I thought you'd never get here. Hank's been pacing the hallway for the past fifteen minutes."

He wanted to ask if she was as eager to see him as Hank was, but he didn't. He just followed her into the living room that was tastefully yet minimally decorated.

As if she could read his mind, she gestured around the room. "I haven't had much time to decorate, but maybe one of these days …"

"I think it looks nice."

"But plain." She paused. "I need to find some wall art and maybe add a few pillows and throws."

"At least you know what you like."

"Oh, I didn't say that. I have no idea what will look good in here."

He looked around before settling his gaze on her. "Ya know, I'm the same way. Maybe we can find an art gallery or something to get some ideas."

"Sounds good to me." She leaned over, cupped Hank's chin in her hand, and looked him in the eyes. "Now you be a good boy while I'm gone."

He whimpered but never broke the gaze. Finally, Emily straightened up and took a step toward the door. "Let's go before he rips my heart out with that look."

After they got into the truck, they both looked at the window where Hank stood staring at them with his forlorn expression. Brice turned to Emily. "He's making it difficult."

"I know."

"You do realize he's upset about our leaving him."

"Yes, that's obvious."

Brice hesitated before adding, "And some dogs—I'm not saying Hank will do this—but some of them will tear everything up in the house out of boredom."

"Well ..." She shifted in her seat. "I'm not sure what to do. I can't stay home all the time."

"You're right, but maybe ..." He grimaced. "Maybe we should take him with us."

"Are you serious?" He would have said *never mind* if she didn't have such a hopeful look on her face.

"Positive. Why don't you go get him while I make a place in the backseat? I have an old blanket he can sit on."

It didn't take her more than a couple of seconds for her to scramble out of the truck and run up to the house. Hank greeted her before she stepped foot inside.

By the time she returned to the truck with Hank, Brice had the blanket laid out on the backseat. Hank jumped right in and positioned himself smack dab in the middle. Brice and Emily buckled themselves in, glanced at each other, and started laughing.

Emily spoke first. "One day I'm footloose and fancy free, but all I do is work. When I take a little time off for myself, I have a dog that needs me more than any of my businesses ever have."

Brice studied her look of amusement. She didn't appear the least bit upset or annoyed by her situation.

"We'll be somewhat limited by where we can go now," she continued. "I hope you don't mind."

"I don't mind at all. I'm pretty sure there are a few dog-friendly places in Raleigh, and I just happen to know of one restaurant that has outdoor seating. They even bring bowls of water for dogs."

"Sounds like my kind of place … at least now it is." Emily chuckled as she shook her head. "Funny how until yesterday, I never gave a second thought to things like that."

"I think there'll probably come a time when it'll be second nature to think about Hank."

"Speaking of Hank …" Emily glanced over her shoulder and saw him looking at her, waiting for her to continue. She laughed. "I need to make an appointment with the V-E-T."

Hank whimpered. Emily shot Brice a glance and grimaced.

"Do you think he can spell?"

Brice shrugged. "I don't know if he can spell, but I'm pretty sure he understood what you just said."

Emily reached behind her and gave Hank a pat on the head. "Everything will be fine, big boy, because I'll be right there beside you."

Hank lowered himself to a prone position and placed his chin between his front paws. Emily felt bad that she might have put him in a bad mood.

They made small talk until they got to Raleigh and found a parking place. Brice got out and then stuck his head back in the truck. "Wait right here, and I'll come around to get you and Hank."

Emily turned around, and they both saw that Hank hadn't budged from his spot, but his eyes moved as they followed her movement. "What's wrong, Hank?"

He grunted right when Brice opened the door. Emily stepped out, but Hank wouldn't budge.

Brice and Emily exchanged a glance before looking back at Hank who was still lying down. "C'mon, boy. Don't you want to walk around Raleigh?"

Hank lifted his head, giving Brice one of his mournful look. Then it dawned on him. "I bet he thinks we're going to the V-E-T."

Hank lifted his head and made another whimpering sound that ended in a grunt. Emily patted him on the head. "Poor baby hates to see the doctor. I bet you're right. We need to do something to make him want to get out."

"Just a second. I might have something." Brice ran around to the back of the truck, pulled down the hinged door, and grabbed one of the squeaky toys that had fallen out of a shipment he'd picked up from one of the local manufacturers.

Emily glanced at the colorful toy in his hand. "What's that?"

"Enticement. If it works to get Hank out, I'll

order a dozen cases of them."

Brice extended it toward Hank, but before the dog could take it, Brice pulled back. Hank glanced at Emily, as if seeking permission.

\

Chapter 7

Emily turned to Brice as they walked down the sidewalk. "I can't believe such a big dog is so enamored with such a little toy."

Brice pointed to Hank who kept closing his teeth over the toy, making it squeak. "I think you've just found his pacifier."

"And you've committed to buying a dozen cases of those toys."

Brice grimaced. "I sure did, didn't I?"

"Yep. And I aim to make sure you follow through. Maybe this will be the hottest new dog trend ever." Emily had to stifle a giggle as she thought about the wide selection of squeaky toys she'd seen at the hardware store as well as every pet aisle in the grocery store.

"Maybe it will be. I'll probably have a pet supply sale soon so I'm not stuck with a dozen boxes of them in the back room."

"Not a bad idea," she said. "Let me know when you run it so I can stock up."

He smiled down at her, causing a flutter in her abdomen. "I'll even start the sale early for you. It'll be a pre-sale sale, just for special friends."

Hank chomped down on the toy, emitting a loud squeak, showing his support. Then he looked up at the two of them with the most comical expression Emily had seen yet. Both Emily and Brice cracked up.

"He is about the funniest thing I've ever seen." Emily sighed. "I don't think I've ever laughed so hard as I have since I've had him."

"I know. Me too." A pensive expression crossed his face.

"What are you thinking?"

He shrugged. "Several things, like maybe I should get a dog, but I know not all of them are as good as Hank. I need to take more time off work." He paused, stopped, and turned Emily to face him. "And I'd like to spend some of that time with you."

Her heart pounded so hard she was sure he could hear it. She smiled and slowly nodded. "I'd like that very much."

"Well, good." He cleared his throat, motioned toward the sidewalk ahead, and resumed walking. "Now that we've settled that, let's get on with our day."

They walked around Raleigh for a little more than an hour before they came upon a smoothie shop with outdoor seating. "Let's take a little break now and get something delicious."

Brice ordered a banana mango smoothie, and Emily chose one with pineapple and papaya. As they sipped their drinks, Hank sat beside the table and watched the people who passed by. Emily couldn't remember ever being so relaxed and satisfied with anything that wasn't work related.

"Penny for your thoughts," Brice said after a few moments of silence.

She tilted her head and gave him a smile. "Only a penny? Haven't you heard about inflation?"

He made an issue of digging into his pocket and pulling out a dime. "How's this?"

"Well ..." She nodded. "I think it's close enough to keeping up with inflation."

"Okay, then." He shoved the dime toward her. "A dime for your thoughts."

Emily didn't want to tell him she was already crazy about him—that he had the demeanor and ready smile that gave her a confusing sensation of being relaxed and on edge at the same time. She didn't want to share that she hadn't been able to take her mind off him ever since meeting him. And she certainly didn't want to let him know she'd never felt that way about a guy so early in a relationship.

"You don't have to tell me if it's that upsetting." He paused and grinned. "But you may keep the dime."

"It's not upsetting. It's just that I'm not sure where to begin."

"Try the beginning. That's always a good place to start."

"I've been thinking about how much I've

enjoyed Hank in the short time I've had him."

"That makes two of us," Brice agreed. "And I don't even have to feed him."

She laughed. "True. And that brings me to another thought. I can't help but wonder if he'll continue to be such a joy."

Brice folded his arms and leaned back in his chair. "We'll know soon enough."

The fact that he used the word *we* caused her voice to catch. She cleared her throat. "And I've been thinking about how much fun I'm having today … with you."

"Me too." He slowly shook his head. "And we're not even doing anything all that exciting. I think some people would expect more from a day off." He leaned forward and placed his hand on top of hers. "I think it's the company. I enjoy being around you, Emily."

Hank chose that moment to let out a, "Woof," and then he placed his own paw on top of their hands. The sound of other people's laughter around them caught their attention.

The woman sitting with a man at the table next to theirs spoke up. "That is about the sweetest thing I think I've ever seen."

Emily smiled at the couple. "Hank is a sweet dog."

"He's so in tune to you." The woman glanced at the man and then at Emily. "In fact, so is your husband. The three of you make a very sweet family."

Emily was speechless, and she wanted to crawl right under the table. But Brice spoke up to take the attention away from her.

"Thank you. It's such a beautiful day, we thought we'd take the dog out to enjoy it with us."

He chatted with the couple for a few minutes until the server came with the check. Emily reached for it, but Brice beat her to it. "My treat," he said with no hesitation.

Emily slowly pulled her hand back as he pulled out his wallet. After the server took payment, they left.

"I hope I didn't embarrass you when I didn't correct that lady," Brice said as they rounded the corner.

"No, not at all."

"I think we make a great threesome." He took her by her free hand. "We need to do this more often."

Her heart felt as though it might explode. "Sounds good to me."

"Look." He pointed to a vintage looking pet store with a sign stating that everyone was welcome, including those with four legs. "Maybe we can find something Hank likes there."

"Oh, I'm sure." Based on Emily's observations of Hank so far, there wasn't much he didn't like, except the vet.

As soon as they walked into the store, Hank's ears started twitching, and his eyebrows shot up. The man who worked there came around from behind the counter, holding up a dog treat. "Is it okay if I give him this?"

Emily nodded. As the man handed Hank the treat, Brice squeezed her hand and turned to the man. "I think you've just made a friend for life."

The man laughed. "I've never met a dog that didn't like coming in here."

Hank agreed by letting out a, "Woof."

"Feel free to look around. If you have any questions, I'll be right here." The man started for the counter but stopped and added, "And don't feel obligated to buy anything. I want my shop to be fun for pets and their people."

After he was out of hearing distance, Brice leaned over and whispered, "I can't imagine leaving this store empty-handed. This place is awesome."

Emily nodded toward Hank who had already begun to browse one of the shelves nearby. "He certainly thinks so."

An hour later, they headed back to the car to put their stash of an oversized dog bed, a couple more dog toys, a bag of all natural, locally made chewy treats, a small bag of dog food that Brice insisted on getting, even though Emily said they didn't need it, and a new collar. Hank seemed perkier than ever.

"Just like a kid," Brice said. "He's really happy about all his new stuff."

"So am I." Emily sighed, as she now understood why parents did what they did to make their children happy. "It's fun to see him so cheerful."

They walked around for another hour before Brice asked if she was hungry. She nodded. "I just hope Hank isn't starving."

"Wait'll you see where we're going. They have a great outdoor dining area, and they allow dogs to eat, as long as you bring food." He lifted a small bag. "That's why I wanted to get the dog food for Hank. I forgot to bring some from the hardware store."

The rest of the day was like a fairy tale for Emily. She had to pinch herself a couple of times to make sure she wasn't dreaming.

By the time Brice brought her and Hank home, she had no doubt she could quickly fall in love with the man. He helped her to the door with all the items she'd bought, and he surprised her with a bracelet she'd admired in one of the stores.

"I didn't see you get that." She held out her arm for him to put it on her. "How did you do that?"

He gave her a goofy grin and wiggled his eyebrows. "I'm sneaky like that."

"Thank you so much for a wonderful day."

Brice took both of Emily's hands in his and looked at her in a way that she never remembered experiencing. "I'm the one who should thank you. You saved me from falling deeper into the workaholic hole."

She slowly nodded. "I think we just saved each other."

"So when would you like to do this again?"

Emily pondered that for a few seconds. "After tomorrow, I'm booked for the next week. I've been working on a few projects, and it looks like they're finally coming to fruition."

He frowned, but he quickly tried to cover it with a smile. "I understand. Do you want to call me when you're free?"

She couldn't help but notice the formality of

his tone. "Sure, but you can call me too."

"But you're so busy." Brice licked his lips and winced. "That came out snarky, didn't it?"

She laughed. "Not really snarky, but—"

He let go of one hand and placed his fingertips over her lips. "It was snarky, and I'm sorry. I was just hoping you had so much fun you couldn't wait to see me again."

"I did have that much fun. And I can't wait to see you again. It's just that I've already committed to some meetings."

Brice pursed his lips and slowly nodded. "Trust me, I understand. Do you have any idea when you'll be free?"

She wanted to tell him tomorrow, but she knew he already felt bad about not being in the store for the big sale. "My last scheduled meeting is on Friday."

"Why don't we plan something for the Saturday after?"

"But you're in the retail business, and Saturday—"

"I know, but I also have some very capable people working for me, including a couple of college students who would love more weekend hours."

"Okay, then. We can get together that Saturday."

"Dinner?"

"Sounds good."

"I'll call you later next week, and we can talk about the details." He gave her hand a squeeze and let go.

She thought he was about to leave, when he leaned over and gave her a quick kiss on the lips. Emily was caught so off-guard, she couldn't think of a thing to say … or do. So she just stood by her front door and watched him walk to his truck, get in, and back out of the driveway.

"Woof." Hank gave her a forlorn expression.

Emily giggled. "My sentiments, exactly. Where were you when I needed you?"

Hank tilted his head and gave her a curious look. She laughed, so he tilted his head the other way and put his paw on her leg.

"What is it with you, Hank? You're just a puppy, but you seem so grown up and human sometimes."

He made a playful pounce on his front paws and then ran off to get a squeaky toy. He brought it to her, dropped it at her feet, and then went to his basket and got another one.

The end of the week couldn't come soon enough. Emily managed to work through her entire list and make all her appointments. In the past, she would have had a tremendous feeling of accomplishment, but now she felt empty. By the time Saturday rolled around, she was more than ready to see Brice.

After he kissed her goodnight at the door, he cupped her face in his hands. "Do I have to wait another whole week to see you again?"

She shook her head. "Not if you want to go to church with me in the morning."

He grinned down at her. "I thought you'd never ask."

Over the next several weeks, they went out on Saturday nights, to church on Sundays and out to lunch afterward. And they took turns coming up with something to do a couple other nights during the week. Emily was starting to get comfortable in the relationship, and Hank was over-the-moon happy when they were all together. Unfortunately, she had to schedule a bunch of appointments close together in one week. "Looks like we'll have to wait until the weekend."

"How about lunch on Wednesday?" He tipped her chin up. "You have to have lunch anyway, so why not have it with me?"

She shook her head. "Sorry, but I have lunch appointments every single day during the week."

His shoulders drooped as he backed away and nodded. "I understand."

She wasn't so sure he did, and it broke her heart. There was no doubt in her mind that she was in love with him, and she was pretty sure he felt the same.

Chapter 8

Brice would have gotten together with Emily every single day if she'd been willing and able. But the very thing that drew him to her in the first place—her work ethic—was the very thing that kept that from happening. Still, he was certain that the next several days would drag. At least he had the business and his civic duties on the town council.

Throughout the next day, he went back and forth between ordering merchandise, meeting with new vendors, helping customers, and following up on parade business. Mooreville typically had forty or fifty groups in the parade, but after how well received last year's event was, it seemed that everyone wanted to be in it.

One of his younger employees, Jonathan, laughed about it. "If everyone's in the parade, who will be there to watch it?"

Brice nodded his agreement. "Good point."

"Speaking of the parade, my mom wants to know if you need more help stuffing the store's float."

"Please let her know we can use all the help we can get."

"My little brother's gonna be happy. He thinks this place is the bomb."

"If he comes, I'll put him in charge of watching the refreshments." Brice forced himself to maintain a straight face. "If I remember correctly, your little brother's favorite thing was the pizza."

"Yeah, he never had pineapple pizza before, and now that's all he ever wants to eat."

"Then I'll make sure we have plenty when it comes time to get the float ready."

Melba approached from the side and held out the phone. "It's for you, boss."

Brice took the phone and gave her a questioning look. She turned around and walked back to the cash register, so he had no idea who was on the line.

"Brice Johnson here. How may I help you?"

"This is Emily Moore, and you may help me by coming to see Hank."

"Huh?" He understood the Emily part, but seeing Hank?

She let out a laugh that made him feel all strange inside, so he turned away from the employees who remained nearby. "Everyday when I come home, he keeps looking around, like he expects to see someone else." She paused. "I'm pretty sure that someone else is you."

"Really?" He wasn't sure what to say, so he didn't say anything.

"Yes, really. I know I told you I was busy until next weekend, but is it possible to stop by soon … at least to see Hank?"

"Um, I think I can manage that." He was tempted to leave right now, but he didn't want to make a fool of himself with her or the people who worked for him. "When?"

"How about tonight? I'm waiting for a meeting now, but I'll be home around seven."

"Want me to bring dinner?"

"You don't have to do that. I just want you to come and spend a little time with Hank. I think he's confused that you're not here."

"I know I don't have to bring anything, but I'd like to." He cleared his throat. "That is, unless you already have dinner plans."

"I don't, but I don't want you going to a lot of trouble."

"How about something from the deli? That's no trouble at all. I'll pick up some sandwiches and chips, and you can supply the drinks. How's that?"

"Gotta run. I'll see you at seven."

After he got off the phone, he saw that all his employees were watching him. "What?"

Jonathan glanced at Melba, who winked and gestured toward Brice. "The look of love."

"We're friends. Her dog is looking around for me, and since she's only had him a short time, I want to help her out." He saw how everyone rolled their eyes. "That's what you do for friends, right?

You help them out."

"Oh yeah. I like to help my friends." Jonathan cleared his throat.

"Sometimes *friends* need more than help with their dogs," Melba said before turning toward the register. "If you need any help or advice, don't hesitate to ask. I have experience with *friends*. In fact, I married my best friend about twenty years ago, so I know what I'm talking about."

Brice heard her message loud and clear. And it didn't bother him in the least. Having more than a friendship with Emily could be a good thing, but if her busyness was any indication of how things would go, he wasn't sure if it was even possible. She was the only person he knew who had more on her plate than he did.

The rest of the day went by quickly, as it always did when they ran specials on things everyone wanted in the spring, like HVAC filters, garden supplies, and flowers. He was in the middle of moving some palettes around when Melba approached.

He looked over at her. "Need something?"

"Yep. I need you to leave this place so you can get ready for your date." Melba folded her arms and gave him one of her motherly looks.

"It's not exactly a date. I'm just dropping by to see Hank because he misses me."

"That's what she told you." Melba tilted her head as she held her gaze.

"She's not one to play games."

Melba shook her head. "I'm not saying she's playing games, but think about it, Brice. Did Hank tell her he wanted to see you?"

"Of course not. He's a dog."

"How does Emily know he wants to see you?"

"He was looking around."

Melba rolled her eyes and laughed. "She wants to think Hank's looking for you … and he very well may be. But she can't be sure."

"Hank is easy to read. I think she can tell."

She made a face. "Perhaps you're right. You said y'all bought him a bunch of new things. Maybe he's looking for more stuff." She tilted her face forward and looked at him from beneath hooded eyebrows. "C'mon, Brice. She wants to see you, and she's using Hank to get you to stop by because she doesn't want to admit her feelings—to you or herself."

Brice chewed his lip for a moment as he realized Melba had a good point. But he wasn't ready to admit that he thought Emily might want to see him as much as he wanted to see her. "I'm going to go see Hank, *just in case* I'm what he's looking for."

"Okay, I can go along with that." Melba stepped closer.

"I've picked out a few things Hank might like, including one of the extra large rawhides you ordered."

Brice's face heated up. He wondered if Melba realized he'd ordered those after meeting Hank.

He decided to knock off a little early after that conversation. On his way out the door, he picked up the package of rawhides and another squeaky toy for Hank. Of all the things in the dog's toy basket, he clearly preferred the ones that made noise.

After a quick shower, Brice texted Emily to find out what kind of sandwich she wanted. To his surprise, she got back with him right away and asked if he minded getting pizza instead. "I've been craving it all day."

"I usually crave it when I'm exhausted."

"Maybe that's why. I'm used to working long hours, but before I had Hank, I could come home and relax. That's pretty much impossible now. I thought we'd go for a short walk when I got home, but he's already become the most popular guy on the block. I can't even take him for a walk without someone stopping us and wanting to talk ... or play with him."

Brice chuckled. "He is a pretty jovial guy. Why don't you relax, and I'll be there as soon as I have the pizza. What do you like on it?"

"Everything."

"Me too. I'll get a deluxe supreme."

As soon as they hung up, he called Bubba Fiore's Pizzeria, his favorite pizza place that he had on speed dial. "Hey, Bubba, this is Brice Johnson. I'd like the usual to go, only this time make it a deluxe size."

"Sure thing, Brice. Going to a party?"

"Nah, just hanging out with a friend."

Bubba laughed. "That friend doesn't just happen to have a dog named Hank, does she?"

"What?" Brice let out a snort. "Where have you heard that?"

"This is Mooreville. People talk."

"Okay, so yes, I'm going to see Hank."

"Good deal. I'll throw in a few treats for the dog. You know that'll earn you a few extra points with the girl, right?"

Brice knew better than to argue with Bubba. "Thanks."

"Just make sure you invite me to the wedding." Brice heard Bubba's deep belly laugh as he clicked the OFF button on his phone.

He got out of the truck and went into the grocery store to get soda. Since he wasn't sure what kind she preferred, he came out with four two-liter bottles.

By the time he arrived at the pizzeria, his order was coming out of the oven. Bubba held up his index finger. "All I have to do is cut it and slide into a box. It'll just be a few shakes of a donkey tail ... or should I say doggie tail?" Bubba let out another deep laugh.

Chapter 9

Emily didn't have to worry about missing the doorbell with Hank around. He ran to the foyer and stared at the door several seconds before she heard the footsteps on the front porch.

She flung the door open and caught Brice trying to figure out how to ring the doorbell while holding a pizza and a large grocery bag. "Saved by the dog."

He looked down at Hank. "You got that right. I owe you a belly rub."

"Woof." Hank took a step back, never breaking his gaze.

"I bet he smells the pizza," Brice said.

"Oh, I'm sure."

"Do you think he's hungry?"

Emily tilted her head forward and gave him a you've-got-to-be-kidding look. "He's always hungry."

Brice laughed. "I have some treats for him too."

"Not pizza."

He shook his head. "That's right. Not pizza. Bubba gave me some goodies for the dog." Brice placed the pizza and bag on the counter and started pulling out the bottles. He reached into his jacket pocket and pulled out the pack of dog treats.

"Whoa." Emily couldn't believe how many treats were in the pack. "That's a lot of dog biscuits."

"That's because he knows all about Hank and how big he is."

"Did you tell him?"

Brice tightened his jaw for a moment and then slowly shook his head. "No, I didn't have to say a word. He knew. In fact, he's been hearing a lot through the Mooreville grapevine."

"Like what?" Emily propped her elbow on the counter and studied Brice's face. He looked annoyed.

"Like he's heard that you and I are ... well, that we're an item."

Emily couldn't help but frown. She hated gossip. "Did he tell you exactly what he'd heard?"

Brice shook his head. "I'm afraid you might not like it." He told her the entire conversation. "I wish people would quit jumping to conclusions when there's not even an ounce of truth to any of it."

Her heart sank. Although she hated people talking about her behind her back, she didn't mind what they were saying since it was pretty much what she'd allowed herself to think about nonstop over the past couple of days.

"Ready for your first slice of pizza?"

"Sure." As she got a couple of plates down from the shelf, she was happy to have a diversion so he wouldn't notice the disappointment on her face. She hated the fact that his simple comment bothered her so much.

"Are you okay?" He took the plate as she handed it to him without looking him in the eyes.

"I'm fine." She pulled a couple of glasses from another shelf and filled them with ice from the door of the refrigerator, continuing to avoid meeting his gaze. Then she handed him one.

He pointed to the lineup of bottles. "I wasn't sure which one you like, so I got several."

She smiled and pointed to the ginger ale. "I don't drink much soda, but when I do, it's usually ginger ale."

He gave her an odd look. "Me too. This is really strange."

"Strange?" She paused and met his gaze. "How?"

"We have so many similarities, it's uncanny."

"I'm sure we have as many differences as similarities." Emily paused as she realized he'd just voiced her thoughts. "We just haven't found them yet."

He poured both of them some ginger ale, lifted his glass, and smiled. "Here's to having fun figuring out what makes us different."

Hank wedged himself between them and made one of his comical faces. Then he lifted his head to look at the pizza.

"Uh oh. He can reach that." Brice pushed the box away from the edge of the counter. "We need to keep an eye on the pizza, or we might not get seconds."

"Watch this." Emily turned to Hank, snapped her fingers to get his attention away from the pizza, and spoke in a firm tone. "No."

Hank took a step back from the counter and gave her a look that melted her heart. But she had to be strong, or she'd lose this battle and possibly more in the future since he'd see that she wasn't serious.

She glanced at Brice, who gave her a thumbs-up, and then turned back to Hank. "Living room."

Hank let out a sigh before slowly walking away from the kitchen. Emily smiled up at Brice.

His look showed that he was clearly impressed. "That was good."

"I know."

"Have y'all been to obedience training already?"

She shook her head. "I found some YouTube videos on how to train a dog."

"That's amazing." He gestured toward their plates. "Let's eat before it gets cold."

Emily had practiced a few simple obedience words with Hank, but she was surprised that the dog had caught on so quickly. And now she was even more surprised that he remained in the living room. That worried her.

She pushed her chair back. "I think I'll get another slice of pizza, but first I need to see what

Hank's up to."

"Yeah, good idea."

When she got to the entrance of the living room, she was relieved that nothing was ripped or shredded. However, all of Hank's toys were scattered over the living room floor.

Brice came up from behind and laughed. "Looks like he had a hard time deciding which toy to play with."

She grimaced. "I hate clutter."

"I'm not surprised." Brice looked around the room before locking gazes with her. "But it's a whole lot better than it could have been."

"I know. I still think I need to work on him a bit."

"Work on him?" Brice leaned back. "What do you mean?"

"I can't have this mess in my house. Hank has a few things to learn, but I'm sure it'll come in time." She paused. "I like everything in its place."

The look on Brice's face changed. "So everything has to be just right in your world?"

She slowly nodded. "Yes, pretty much."

Now his expression clouded over. Emily was pretty sure that what she said bothered him, but it was the truth. She'd been on her own for so long that she liked everything done a certain way, or she wasn't happy.

They ate their pizza in silence, until Brice finally stood up. "It's time for me to do what I came here for, and that's to give Hank some attention." He started for the living room but stopped and glanced at her over his shoulder. "I'll clean up his mess so you won't have to deal with it after I leave."

Emily remained seated at the table. On the one hand, she wanted to hop up and tell him he'd misunderstood. On the other hand, she was who she was, and she didn't want to make excuses or lie.

She listened to Brice talk to Hank about being a good dog. When he stopped talking, she assumed he'd started straightening up the room—something she didn't think he should feel responsible for. So she hopped up and joined them. She was right. Brice was on the floor, picking up all the toys and tossing them into the basket.

She cleared her throat. "You don't need to do that."

He glanced up. "I don't want you getting mad at Hank for being a puppy." He moved over to another area and started picking more toys.

"I'm not mad." She crossed the room and stood next to him. "Please don't do this. I'm sorry if I came across angry."

Brice's shoulders rose and fell as he took a deep breath. "Hank's a good dog. I'd much rather see him dig out all his toys and scatter them around your house than tear up your furniture. He's still a puppy, and you can't expect—"

"I know," she interrupted. "And I don't expect anything from him."

"But you said—" He cut himself off. "Never mind."

She tilted her head and looked at him for a few seconds before Hank came up, sat next to her and leaned into her side. She patted his head.

Brice tossed the last of the squeaky toys into the basket and stood up. "I think it's time for me to go now."

Hank let out another, "Woof," before standing up and walking over to Brice. He placed his paw on Brice's thigh.

Brice gave Hank a scratch between the ears. "You're a good dog, Hank."

The mood had grown so dark, Emily thought it was time to lighten up. "I bet you wish you'd seen him before I did."

Brice didn't offer even a hint of a smile. Instead, he shook his head. "No, I think things worked out the way they were supposed to."

Emily detected something deeper beyond the subject, but his tone of finality kept her from pressing. She followed him down the long hallway toward the front of the house.

He opened the door and stepped out onto the porch. "Thanks for letting me see Hank. He's really a good dog."

"I know." She forced a smile, in spite of the heaviness she felt in her chest. "I overreacted."

He met her gaze but didn't mention her reaction. Instead, he said, "Thank you for letting me see Hank."

As she remained standing at the door watching him leave, she wanted to say something but had no idea what. For the first time in her life, she was speechless … and she wanted a do-over.

The next morning, Emily woke up to a face staring down at her. Who needed an alarm when Hank was around?

"Hungry?"

He whimpered and headed to her bedroom door, glancing over his shoulder a couple of times. Then he let out his familiar, "Woof."

"You need to go out, don't you?" She tossed back the covers, sat up, and stretched. "Let me put some clothes on, and I'll take you for a walk."

She pulled on some sweatpants and an oversized T-shirt, stuffed her phone in her pants pocket, and grabbed a pair of her old gardening sneakers on her way to the door. Hank had already gotten his leash off the hook and stood in the foyer waiting for her. She couldn't help but laugh.

It was a beautiful spring day, something Emily might not have noticed if it weren't for Hank getting her up so early. Normally, she'd wake up about an hour later, grab a cup of coffee to go, and head out to her first appointment without even looking up at the sky. Now she had a few minutes to actually take a breath and enjoy the sunshine and buds that had begun to form on the trees.

She'd barely made it around the block when her cell phone rang. Since she didn't recognize the number, she considered not answering it, but that went against her nature. So she clicked the ON button.

"Hi, Emily. How's Hank doing?" It was Mr. Friedman. "Has he eaten you out of house and home yet?"

Emily laughed. "Not yet, but he's only been with me a few days."

"I hope you're happy with him, but if you're

not, you can always bring him back."

"Are you asking for him back?"

"No, of course not. I just don't want you to feel like you're stuck with him if things aren't working out."

She thought about how different things had been since she'd had him. Her life was a tad messier than it used to be, but it wasn't anything she couldn't handle.

"Everything's working out just fine." She paused for a second, and something dawned on her. "Did you think something was wrong?"

"Um … not really." His hesitation let her know he wasn't telling the whole truth.

"What's going on, Mr. Friedman?"

Chapter 10

Brice had just left the shoe shop and got to the hardware store about five minutes ago, when he realized he'd forgotten his wallet on the counter. "Melba, I'll be right back. I need to go get my wallet."

She smiled and gave him a thumbs-up. "Take your time."

As soon as he rounded the corner, he saw Mr. Friedman through the shop window, talking on the phone. Brice slowed down to give the man a little more time to finish his call.

The instant the bell on the door jangled, Mr. Friedman glanced up and started to welcome him, until he realized it was Brice. Then a guilty look overtook his smile.

"What can I do for you?" Mr. Friedman came around from behind the counter and stood with his hands on his hips.

Brice pointed. "I left my wallet."

Mr. Friedman glanced at it. "So you did. I didn't even notice."

Brice studied the older man for a few seconds. "I suppose when you're as busy as you are, and you get one call after another, it's hard to notice little details."

The cobbler closed his eyes shook his head. "Okay, so I called her after you left."

"You called *her*?" Brice narrowed his eyes. "Who are you talking about?"

"Emily."

"That's fine. You don't have to tell me who you called."

Mr. Friedman pursed his lips as he ran his fingers through his sparse hair. "But I called her because of something you said. Now I'm embarrassed to admit something I said."

"Why are you embarrassed?" Brice narrowed his eyes. "What did you say?"

Brice watched as Mr. Friedman's expression changed several times, until he finally let out a deep breath and allowed his shoulders to sag. "I was worried after you told me about Emily being upset that Hank strewed his toys all over her house, so I called her and said if she wasn't happy with him, she could bring him back."

"And what did she say?"

"She said everything is just fine." He glanced down at his shoes before looking Brice in the eyes. "She asked me why I thought it might not be."

Brice folded his arms and tilted his head toward

Mr. Friedman. "And what did you tell her?"

The older man grimaced. "The truth."

"Did you mention my name?"

Mr. Friedman slowly nodded. "Yes, and now I'm sorry I ever called her. I meant well, but I'm afraid I came across as a meddlesome old man."

Brice was annoyed by the fact that Mr. Friedman had spoken to Emily, but it only reinforced the fact that he should never say anything to anyone that he didn't want repeated. "Don't worry about it."

"I'm really sorry."

Brice forced a smile. "It's not that big of a deal."

"Maybe not, but ..." Mr. Friedman winced as he shrugged. "I still need to mind my own business."

"You were just checking in on Hank. It's understandable."

"I have to admit I miss that dog. There's something special about him."

Brice agreed. "You're right. He's smart."

"Smart, yes, but it's more than that. He has a special sense that I've never seen in any of my other dogs."

"I'm sure you have something to do with that." Brice backed toward the door. He was angry but more at himself than Mr. Friedman. "I need to get back to the hardware store so Melba can go home."

He'd barely taken a couple of steps when he spotted Emily and Hank walking on the other side of the street. She shifted the leash to her other hand, tucked her hair behind her ears, and kept walking.

He knew he needed to say something, and even though he had no idea what, he decided to take a chance.

"Emily."

She glanced directly at him and lifted her chin. "Hi, Brice."

Hank's ears perked up as he glanced at Emily and then at Brice. "Hey there, Hank." He gave Emily an apologetic smile. "Can we talk?"

She lifted a shoulder in a half shrug. "I don't know."

"Please?" He swallowed and took a deep breath before slowly letting it out. "It's important."

Emily hesitated before tugging on the leash and changing her direction to cross the street toward Brice. Relief flooded him as it became obvious that she wouldn't bolt. Seconds later, she stood a couple of feet away, looking him directly in the eyes. "What did you want to talk about?"

"I want to tell you how sorry I am about talking to Mr. Friedman." He glanced down at his feet and then at her.

"Hey, don't worry about it."

"I'm not worried." The instant those words escaped his mouth he shook his head. "Okay, I lied. I am worried. Very worried."

"It's no big deal." Her icy tone let him know how big of a deal it was. "Really."

"It *is* a big deal. You're upset with me, and you have every right to be." He didn't like this conversation any more than the fact that he'd messed up in the first place. "Can we start over?"

She shrugged. "Sure. Where do you want to

start?"

He smiled and extended his hand. "Hi, I'm Brice Johnson."

Emily glanced at his hand and chuckled. "I'll have to hand it to you, Brice. You don't give up."

"That's right." He pulled back his hand and shoved it into his pocket. "And neither do you, which is something I really like about you."

"Are you serious?" She tilted her head and narrowed her eyes.

"Absolutely. You are at least as tenacious as I am, and that's why you're a success. I'm sure my tenacity is the only reason I'm not working for someone else."

"Okay, that makes sense."

"Would you like to hang out later tonight?"

She shook her head. "No, not tonight. I'm taking Hank to a private obedience class."

"Maybe some other time then?" He gave her a hopeful look.

She gave him a forced smile. "Maybe. See you around, Brice."

He gave her a clipped nod as he realized he'd messed up so badly he might never break through her shell again. She started to leave, when he remembered the Pets on Parade segment of the town's celebration.

"Hey Emily."

She glanced over her shoulder. "What?"

"Don't forget about the parade meeting."

She spun around. "What parade meeting?"

"The one we're having tomorrow night."

A confused look came over Emily. "I don't

remember hearing anything about a parade meeting."

That was because he'd just decided to have one. "It's tomorrow night on the Town Square at 7:00 PM." He nodded toward the dog. "Bring Hank."

"Of course." She pursed her lips. "Is that all?"

Brice nodded. "For now, anyway."

After she disappeared around the corner with Hank, Brice leaned against the corner of the building and rubbed his face. He should have been able to come up with something that wasn't quite as lame as a parade meeting. Now he had to go around and let everyone else know that there was a meeting he hadn't planned. Hopefully, the short notice wouldn't annoy too many people.

To his surprise, the majority of the business owners said they were excited about the meeting. All he had to do now was go home and call the schools and civic organizations to let them know.

The next morning, Brice got up and headed straight for the kitchen. He needed to call in and let his employees know he'd be in late so he could plan the meeting he didn't even know he was having until yesterday afternoon. A couple of his most dedicated employees arrived extra early to accommodate the contractors who needed to get to their worksites.

Melba answered the phone as she always did, her voice laced with laughter. "Hey, boss, what's up? I heard about your chat with Emily. Is that why you've decided to throw in an extra meeting?"

He started to argue, but this woman could read

him too well. "You've got my number, Melba."

"I know I do. I'm about to head out to make a delivery. Mind if I stop by your house for a few minutes?"

Brice really didn't feel like seeing anyone now, but Melba was like a second mother to him. He couldn't turn her down. "Sure, I'll make sure I have a full pot of coffee ready when you get here."

After he hung up, he quickly got ready for the day and then sat down at the kitchen table to work on his plans. He'd barely started his list of what to discuss when he heard the knock at the door. After he let her in, she led the way to the kitchen.

"I'll get my own coffee. You have a seat and finish whatever you were doing."

"Yes, ma'am." He sat down and finished the sentence he'd started before looking up at the only woman besides his mother who could tell him what to do.

"Let me give you a few tips on how to deal with things, now that you've gotten yourself into a pile of pickles."

"Super sour pickles at that."

She grinned. "You said it, I didn't."

Once she joined him at the table, she asked if he was okay. He shrugged, so she leaned forward and began the lecture that he knew he had coming to him.

After she finished, she sat back and looked him up and down. "You look nice today, boss." Then she leaned forward gave him a pat on the shoulder. "Don't blow your chance with this girl. I sense something really special—something that only comes along once in a lifetime." She lifted her coffee mug, took a sip, and stood up. "I need to get back to the store. What time do you think you'll be in?"

Brice glanced at his list. "I don't know. Maybe in an hour or so?"

"Take your time." She tipped her head forward. "I know how you like every minute to count." She glanced at the wall clock. "Speaking of time, I'd better hustle. I don't want to keep anyone waiting."

"Thanks, Melba. I'll see you later this morning."

He walked her to the door and then returned to his planning. It took a whole hour to come up with enough valuable information to justify the meeting.

On the way to the hardware store, he stopped off at the office supply store to make copies of the safety rules for each group—one for the walkers, one for the floats, and another for the people with animals. The guy at the copy center offered to help out with the pets.

"I used to work at the pet store, and I spent quite a bit of time with the trainers."

"Perfect." Brice stacked the papers on the counter. "Can you come to the meeting tonight?"

The man with the nametag that read *Sam* nodded. "I thought you'd never ask."

"Thanks."

"I can even walk with the pets if you want me to."

It hadn't dawned on Brice that he'd need someone to walk with the pets, but now that Sam mentioned it, he thought it was a great idea.

"Absolutely, yes. That'll be a huge help."

Sam beamed. "I'll be there tonight."

Brice left and went straight to the hardware store. Melba waved but continued talking to a customer. Ross and Andrew were in the back of the store, maneuvering a pallet jack to make room for more merchandise.

The rest of the day was normal, with a steady flow of customers, from contractors and do-it-yourselfers to folks who were preparing their gardens. At the end of the day, Brice barely had time to close the store before going straight to the Town Square for the meeting.

He'd brought some of the notes into the store with him so he could prepare for the meeting, but he'd been too busy to look at them. Before leaving the store, he glanced over the notes so he'd have them fresh on his mind.

As soon as Brice rounded the corner to the Town Square, he saw the large crowd of people who'd arrived early. He looked around until his eyes settled on Emily and Hank. She glanced up but didn't smile before turning back to Charlotte, the manager of the skating rink. The tiny bulldog puppy seemed mesmerized by Hank, while the two women were deep in conversation.

He approached them with the biggest smile he could manage. "Good evening, ladies."

Charlotte looked over at him with the saddest eyes he'd ever seen. "I wish."

"What's wrong?"

Her chin quivered, and she took a swipe at her nose with the back of her hand. "I have to find a home for Biscuit."

Chapter 11

Emily didn't know Charlotte well, but she felt for the woman who'd just found out she was being promoted and transferred to the West Coast. Charlotte admitted that until she'd moved to Mooreville, she was ambitious and welcomed every promotion she had. But now, she was settled and enjoyed small-town living.

"I even got a dog." She sniffled. "I don't want to move, but I need my job."

Brice tilted his head. "Why can't you bring Biscuit with you?"

Emily stepped back and let Charlotte answer. "I'll be a district manager, which means I'll be traveling." She sniffled. "A lot."

"I'm so sorry." Brice's forehead crinkled. "Maybe someone here would like to adopt him."

"It would have to be someone super nice …"

Emily glanced down and saw that Hank and Biscuit had found comfortable spots on the grass to lie down next to each other.

Charlotte nodded. "Someone I can trust to take great care of him."

Brice squatted down and scratched both dogs behind the ears. They both leaned into his hands. Everyone was quiet for about a minute, until Brice stood up.

"I have an idea. I'll take him."

Emily and Charlotte both turned to him and spoke in unison. "You will?"

"Yeah." Brice looked just as stunned as Emily was, but he was smiling. "He seems like a really good dog, and he's pretty social. I might even let him hang out with me at the hardware store."

Charlotte's face lit up. "You're right. He's super social, and I think he'd love being in the store."

"Then it's settled." Brice took a step toward the small platform. "When are you moving?"

"The week after the celebration."

"Good. You'll still be able to walk him in the parade. I need to start this meeting so everyone can go home. We'll talk later."

As soon as he was out of hearing distance, Charlotte turned to Emily. "Are you okay with this?"

"What do you mean?"

"I mean, is it okay for your boyfriend to have a dog, since you have Hank?"

Emily's voice caught in her throat, so she cleared it. "First of all, he's not my boyfriend, and second, Biscuit and Hank get along great."

"Wow. Could've fooled me. I thought the two of you were, like, engaged or something."

"They're not yet, but you never know what the future holds." The familiar masculine voice came from behind them.

Emily turned around and made eye contact with Mr. Friedman. "I don't think so. We're, um … friends."

Mr. Friedman smiled at her before exchanging a look with Charlotte who gave him back a conspiratorial grin. Since they didn't exchange words, there was nothing for Emily to deny without sounding guilty.

Brice chose that moment to start the meeting. He began by discussing where everyone would gather, how he'd have a place for personal belongings if they didn't have other arrangements, and where the parade would end. Then he went over the safety rules for everyone before dismissing the marching bands and walkers. Next, he discussed float and car safety and handed out the printouts that were pertinent only to them. After the people from the floats and cars left, he addressed the people who would take up the end of the parade with their dogs. He explained that the dog parents were responsible for picking up after their pets. "I'll have plenty of bags you can carry with you, and there'll be trash cans along the parade route."

After he finished his talk, Charlotte leaned over and whispered, "He's a really sharp guy." She grinned. "And cute too. You might want to rethink this just-friends relationship. I think the two of you are really good together."

"I agree wholeheartedly," Mr. Friedman said. "But what do I know? I'm just a little old man who has been around for decades. I've seen plenty of people get together who shouldn't and others miss out on a good thing when it's being served on a silver platter." He shrugged. "But like I said. What do I know?"

Charlotte gave Emily an apologetic smile but didn't say anything else. Emily just stood there and waited for the crowd to dissipate before saying goodbye to her friend.

Emily was on her way to her car when she heard her name. When she spun around, she saw Brice running toward her.

"Good." He stopped and caught his breath. "I'm glad you haven't left yet."

"Did you need something?" Being around Brice again, after she'd had time to gather her thoughts, made her want to forget the disagreement had happened. The problem was that she knew it would happen again.

"Can we talk?"

"About what?" She saw his discomfort. "I don't think we have much else to say, unless you need help with the parade."

"I do need help." He reached out and touched her arm. "With the parade … and with my attitude. I think we need to work through a few things."

She shrugged. "I don't know, Brice. You said it yourself. Everything in my world has to be just right."

"Maybe that's because there's something

important missing from your life."

"What could that be?" She tightened her grip on the leash and planted her other fist on her hip as she gave him a challenging stare.

"Me."

"You?"

He nodded. "Just think about it, Emily. We get along great. We understand each other because we're so similar, we both like dogs—"

"I'm sorry, but that's not enough."

"Wait. I'm not finished." He paused, took a deep breath, and blurted, "There's something special between us—something I can't quite put my finger on." He held her gaze long enough to take her breath away. "I think I'm falling in love with you."

Emily's chin dropped, and she found herself speechless. No one had ever told her that before.

"How about it? Can we at least try to work things out?"

"I don't know."

"Please give me a chance."

She closed her eyes and imagined all that could go wrong and how painful that would be. But then what if they could work through the problems? Was she willing to risk the possibility of a broken heart for the opportunity to have something special with a man she couldn't stop thinking about? She'd never been one to throw caution to the wind.

"Let me think about it, okay?"

He smiled. "That's all I can ask. In the meantime, do you mind if I stop by and pick you up on my way to dinner tonight?" His smile faded as he looked down and kicked the ground. "What I mean is, can we go somewhere for dinner so we can talk?"

One thing about him, he was persistent. She sighed. "That's fine."

"This time, we'll need to leave Hank at home. I don't think dogs are welcome where we're going."

Emily's stomach churned, as she got ready for dinner with Brice. At first she couldn't believe how easily she had given in, but after thinking about it, she realized this was exactly what she really wanted—another chance. However, she needed to make it clear that he couldn't change her.

Finally, after she finished putting on her earrings, she stepped back from the full-length mirror and took a long look at herself. She saw something different on her face. It wasn't the confident expression she normally wore. It was more of a look of wonder bordering on confusion. Well, that's how it is, take it or leave it.

Brice arrived precisely when he told her he'd be there. She bent over, cupped Hank's chin in her hands, and spoke softly but in the sternest voice she could. "Behave while I'm gone, and I'll give you a treat when I get back."

He looked right back at her, and when she let go, he emitted his, "Woof."

She smiled, nodded, and straightened up. "Good boy. I think you understand."

As soon as she opened the front door, Brice handed her a bouquet of flowers. "From my garden," he said.

The last time she'd gotten flowers from a guy was back in high school, and they were in the form of a corsage. "Thank you."

"You're welcome."

She carried the flowers back to her kitchen, while Brice hung out at the front of the house with Hank. When she got back, she caught Brice speaking softly to the dog. He looked up at her with a guilty expression.

"What are you telling him?"

"It's just guy talk. Nothing you need to know about."

She was surprised when he drove straight to the Mooreville Diner. "We're eating here?"

"I figured you didn't want to be away from Hank too long, and this was the closest place."

"Okay." It made sense. "I'll just ask my cousin for a doggie bag before we leave. He always has a soup bone in the fridge."

"Perfect. I'm sure Hank will love that."

As they found a booth in the very back corner, Emily thought about how it didn't matter where they were. For the first time in her adult life, she had a sense that anyplace would be special when she was with Brice.

"Let's slay the elephant in the room before we discuss anything else," he said as soon as they ordered. "Because I have a feeling we won't be able to move forward unless we do."

"You really think we need to talk about that now?"

"C'mon, Emily, you know we do. Both of us are no-nonsense people who can run our own businesses with one hand tied behind our back. Let's get this cleared up and then resume getting to know other things about each other.

She nodded. He was right. She liked him, and he obviously liked her. Unfortunately, they both liked having their way because they'd never had to give in. That was the only thing that could prevent them from having a decent relationship.

As they talked, she discovered some things about him that she recognized in herself. They'd both been dreamers as children, as most kids were. The only difference between them and others was that no one could convince either of them that their dreams weren't attainable.

"People tried to warn me how big and bad the world was," she admitted, "but I wouldn't listen."

"I know. Same here." He told her about some of the things his aunts and uncles had said. "But my grandparents encouraged me and even gave me the starting capital for my first business."

"They did?"

"Yep. They handed me a twenty dollar bill and said it was their investment in my future."

Emily laughed. "You made it sound like they gave you a fortune."

"It was a fortune for an up-and-coming lemonade stand operator. With the twenty bucks from them and the free cups and lemonade mix from my parents, I could do anything."

After they finished their dinner, Brice looked at his watch. "Let's get on back before Hank decides we've been gone too long. I think if we take this in small strides and gradually increase the time we're away, we won't have a problem with him getting bored and doing bad stuff."

"We?"

He nodded. "That's what I said."

When he pulled into her driveway, they both noticed Hank watching for them from the front window. His comical expression was lit by the streetlights.

As soon as he realized it was them, he jumped down from the sofa and ran toward the door. Right when she unlocked the door, he started jumping around and running in circles.

She held up the bag. "Ready for your treat?"

Hank gestured toward the back of the house. "Let's check and make sure he didn't wreck the place first."

"Oh, that's right."

As they walked through the house, the only thing they noticed was that he'd pulled out a few of his toys. When they got back toward the front, Brice pointed to the sofa. Hank had pulled his blanket and a stuffed monkey up there.

"That is so sweet." Emily sighed. "Okay, Hank, you were a very good boy."

She pulled out the soup bone and held it out to him. He took one sniff, gently took it from her, and carried it to the kitchen.

Brice tilted his head. "How did he know to go in there?"

"I told you, I've been working with him." She smiled back. "He's a fast learner."

"So am I." Brice grinned as he pulled her closer, gave her a quick kiss on the lips, and let go.

"I'll call you tomorrow."

Three weeks later, Emily stood in the crowd, holding tight to Hank's leash. She'd taken him into the pet store and picked out a cool bandana that showed off his handsome face. Charlotte stood beside her with Biscuit.

"I was starting to fall in love with this place," Charlotte said. "It's hard to believe I'll be living in Seattle in less than two weeks."

"That's what you get for doing such a good job."

"The skating rink challenge wasn't as difficult as I thought it would be, thanks to the town council for supporting it."

A wave of sadness washed over Emily. She still didn't know Charlotte very well, but she had a feeling they would have become very good friends if given the time. "You can stay with me when you come back to visit."

"Thanks." Something behind Emily caught Charlotte's attention.

Emily spun around to see Brice taking long strides toward them, making her heart race even faster than the first time she realized she was attracted to him. She and Brice had done something practically every single day since that night at her cousin's diner. Sometimes they took Hank, and other times they went without him. They always rewarded him for good behavior, which had become the norm.

"When are you bringing Biscuit over?" Hank asked.

"Whenever you want me to. I have to pack my place and get it ready for the movers, so it's probably a good idea to do it soon."

Brice nodded. "How about I take him home with me after the parade to save you the trip?"

Charlotte hesitated only for a few seconds before nodding. "Sure, that's probably a good idea."

Brice squatted down and rubbed Biscuit's head. "You and I are gonna hang out and be best buddies. I've already got you a bed next to mine, and you'll love the cool fountain-style water bowl I've set up in the kitchen."

"You're going to spoil him." Charlotte made a face. "He has to sleep on an old blanket at my place, and the water bowl … well, it's just a plastic bowl I got at the dollar store."

Emily laughed. "You don't have to worry a second about Biscuit being taken care of. I've seen the setup, and it's even nicer than he's telling you."

"I just hope he doesn't forget about me."

Brice shook his head. "He won't." He stood up and gestured toward the rest of the people in the parade. "I need to go get this thing started. If you need anything, Sam will be right there walking with the group. Have fun." He gave a mock salute. "See you after the parade."

As soon as he left, Charlotte leaned over and whispered, "I'm so glad y'all are back together. I know you said you weren't an item, but I could tell."

Emily didn't say anything back. She simply nodded.

"Oh, and the fact that these two get along so

well ..." She motioned toward Hank and Biscuit who were sitting and leaning toward each other. "It gives me even more peace of mind." She smiled before adding, "And hope."

Sam stepped up to the dog group. "Okay, folks. It's time. Let's get these puppies on parade started."

As they walked their dogs through town, past all the people who'd lined up along the sidewalks, Emily and Charlotte talked about everything from business to life in Mooreville. By the time they reached the end, they'd shared most of their life stories.

Brice approached and gave Charlotte a questioning look. She held out the leash, and as he took it, she sighed. "I'm so happy he has you to go home with." Then she turned to Emily. "And I look forward to having you visit me in Seattle sometime soon." She gave Emily a hug. "I'd better go now before I start blubbering."

After she left, Brice closed the distance between himself and Emily. "Are you okay?"

"Yeah, but just a little sad about the fact that my new best friend is leaving."

"Tell you what. Whenever you want to visit her, I can watch Hank. I'm sure Biscuit will love having a house guest."

Emily put her arms around Brice's neck and gave him a kiss on the cheek. This was the first time in her entire life she'd initiated a show of public affection, but it seemed natural.

An odd expression came over him, and it seemed as though time had stood still. "I love you, Emily."

"I love you too."

Epilogue

Six months later, Emily stood in the back of the church, peeking around the corner at Brice who stood at the altar with a dog on each side and a row of groomsmen standing nearby. She couldn't believe that she was actually getting ready to commit her life to this man who she'd almost given up on before giving him a chance.

"Ready, Em?"

She turned to face her dad. "As ready as I'll ever be."

"Then let's get going. The dogs are being good so far, so let's not push their patience."

Emily laughed. The day after she accepted his proposal, they decided to have the dogs in the wedding.

It was initially Brice's idea. "They'll add a little comic relief, so we won't feel so much pressure."

"And we won't have to work on some silly dance routine that'll wind up on YouTube."

After her dad handed her over to Brice, both dogs behaved as they'd been taught. She and Brice said their vows, listened as the pastor pronounced them husband and wife, and then gave each other a big old kiss in front of the entire congregation.

Before they headed back up the aisle, Hank let out a resounding, "Woof!" Then little Biscuit started barking.

"Sshh." Emily couldn't help but laugh. "Don't y'all remember you're not supposed to do that in church?"

"At least they waited until we said our vows." Brice kissed her forehead. "Ready to get the reception thing over with so we can head out to Seattle?"

"Ready as ever."

The rest of the day was a blur to Emily. She'd had a fulfilling career that she planned to return to, only it would be better than ever, now that she had the ideal husband, a best friend who was almost as excited as she was, and a couple of dogs who would make sure there was never a dull moment.

The End

Keep reading for the first chapter of Kittens for Keeps

Dear Reader,

I hope you enjoyed *Puppies on Parade* as much as I loved writing it. Please take a couple of minutes to leave an honest review on Amazon or Goodreads.

Thanks!
Debby Mayne

More books by Debby Mayne:

Trouble in Paradise (contemporary romance – first book in the Belles in the City series)
Julia's Arranged Marriage (historical romance – first book in the Hollister Sisters Mail Order Brides series)
Murder Under the Mistletoe (mystery – first book in the Summer Walsh series)
Kittens for Keeps – a romance with some adorable kittens and a sweet little girl

Please visit my author page for even more books and novellas!

KITTENS FOR KEEPS

Chapter 1

Melissa Hewitt leaned against her kindergarten classroom door and sighed. She loved teaching, but she was tired of going home to an empty apartment. After dating several different men who were clearly not right for her, she'd given up on finding someone to spend the rest of her life with. Either they were too ambitious, too demanding, or too set in their ways. The one time she'd let go of her reservations, she'd been hurt so badly she figured it wasn't worth expecting her own happy-ever-after.

In spite of her parents' offer of moving back in with them, she'd been on her own long enough to know that wasn't such a good idea. She loved being independent, but she was still lonely.

The words of Elaine Masterson, another kindergarten teacher, rang through her head. "Get a kitten. They're great company."

Maybe that's what she should do. She thought about it off and on throughout the afternoon while the kids had free time. She loved animals, and having a kitten made sense. Since all of the children were so engrossed in what they were doing, she decided to take advantage of the time and record some of the skills test scores from that morning.

"Miss Hewitt?"

She glanced up and smiled. "Yes, Ruby?"

The little girl shoved a sheet of paper in front of her. "Do you like the kitty I drew?"

Melissa's mouth went dry as she studied the paper. Ruby's attempt at drawing a cat would have been precious no matter what, but the fact that she'd had kittens on her mind ever since lunch was disconcerting.

"Do you?" Ruby's forehead scrunched as she leaned closer to Melissa.

"Yes, Ruby, it's lovely."

A grin widened Ruby's lips. "Wanna know what her name is?"

"What's her name?" Melissa leaned back and folded her hands over her lap.

"Butter."

Melissa couldn't help but laugh. "Butter?"

"Yes, because she's yellow, and butter is yellow, so that has to be her name."

"You know there are other things that are yellow."

Ruby studied her drawing before turning back to face Melissa. "Like what?"

"Like ..." Melissa thought for a moment. "Like lemons and sunshine and ..." Her voice trailed off as she tried to think of more yellow things.

"Lemons are sour, and kitties are sweet." Ruby contorted her mouth as she looked at her drawing again. "But I like Sunshine. Maybe I'll call her Butter Sunshine."

"Do you have a kitten?" Melissa asked.

The little girls expression darkened. "No, my little brother is 'lergic, so my mommy says I can't have one."

"I'm sorry." Melissa pointed to the paper. "Butter

Sunshine is a pretty name for your drawing."

Ruby's face softened back into a smile as she turned to go back to her place at the long table. "I love Butter Sunshine."

Melissa managed to get all the test scores entered into the computer before the children's free time was over. She let Ruby choose a book to read to the class, and of course the little girl chose one about cats.

By the time the bell rang, Melissa had decided she'd stop by the animal shelter on the way home and see if they had any kittens. She walked the kids to the bus area and then went back into the school to gather everything to go home.

"You look deep in thought."

Melissa glanced up and saw Elaine standing at the door of her classroom. "I've been thinking about what you said."

"What I said?" Elaine stepped into the classroom. "I must be getting old. I can't remember. What did I say, and when did I say it?"

"Remember during lunch, when I was talking about how I go home to an empty apartment everyday, and you said I should get a cat?"

Elaine slowly nodded. "Oh yeah, I remember that. So what are you thinking?"

"I think I just might do that."

"Have you ever had a cat before?" Elaine said. "They're pretty easy, but they still require some care."

"Of course." Melissa made a face. "I know that."

"Just making sure. So if you want to get one, you'll need to have some food and bowls and get a litter pan set up." She paused. "Trust me. I learned the hard way to do that first."

"Okay."

"So when do you plan to get one?"

Melissa shrugged. "I don't know. Maybe I'll stop off at the animal shelter on my way home."

Elaine chuckled. "I didn't realize how persuasive I could be. I barely even mentioned it." She lifted her chin and made a comical face. "Maybe I should be in sales."

"The timing was good." Melissa draped the strap of her handbag over her shoulder and gestured toward the door. "Want to head out together?"

"Sure. I'll just stop by my classroom and get my stuff if you don't mind waiting."

As they walked toward the teacher parking lot, Elaine gave Melissa some advice about getting a cat. "You'll need to get the right food for the age of the cat, and as soon as possible, make a vet appointment."

Melissa frowned. "There's a lot more to having a cat than I realized."

"I know, but it's all totally worth it." Elaine paused when they reached her car. "You might even want to think about getting two of them." She glanced at her watch. "I think the shelter is open a little later today."

"Wait a minute. Two?"

Elaine nodded. "Yeah, so they can keep each other company while you're at work."

"I don't know about two."

"Think about it." Elaine unlocked her car door. "It's just as easy to have two, and they'll be much happier." She paused. "And it's hilarious to watch kittens play with each other."

As Melissa walked the rest of the way to her car, she pondered Elaine's advice. Two cats? She hadn't had a pet since she was a teenager, and that was a dog. She wasn't even sure what it would be like to have a kitten.

On the way to the animal shelter, she noticed one

of the national chain pet stores, so she pulled into the parking lot. Even if she didn't get a cat today, she figured she'd at least need to know how much everything was. By the time she left, she had a big bag filled with kitten food, cat toys, a scratching post, and other things the clerk had convinced her she'd need in one hand and a litter pan in the other. "If you decide not to get a kitten, you can return everything within thirty days," the clerk assured her.

Anticipation rising, Melissa left the pet store parking lot and headed toward the animal shelter. Now that she had all the supplies, the idea of getting a kitten seemed more real.

All Melissa's life, she'd been one to plan things out, all the way down to the last detail, before actually doing anything of any significance. This was the first time she could remember that she'd acted the least bit impulsive. But really, how impulsive was this? She'd been lonely for a while now, and it made sense to get a pet since she'd given up expecting a man to fill the void in her life.

Her heart pounded as soon as she turned onto the street with the animal shelter. It was at the end of a short road. She pulled into the large parking lot, lowered her head momentarily, and asked the Lord for the wisdom to make the best decision.

The walk up to the door seemed to take forever, but once inside, the sounds of dogs barking rattled her nerves a bit. The woman behind the desk grinned. "First time here?"

Melissa nodded. "I'd like to look at some kittens."

"Sign in here." The woman shoved a clipboard toward her. "If you find a kitten you like, you'll need to fill out some paperwork." Her grin widened. "We have a lot of kittens, so I'm sure you'll see at least one you like."

"Miss Hewitt?"

Melissa spun around and saw a little girl she recognized as being one of Elaine's students. "Hi there. Are you getting a new pet?"

The little girl shook her head. "No, my daddy won't let me. He's fixing their website so people can look at animals online."

"Oh." She still didn't know the little girl's name, so she gave the woman behind the desk a curious look, hoping to be clued in.

"Her dad is Mr. Woodall, our IT guy," the woman whispered. "He updates it periodically." She pointed to the clipboard. "As soon as you sign in, I'll have Trent take you back to the cats."

After Melissa signed her name, a young man she assumed was Trent came around from a room behind the desk and gestured for her to follow him. "We have a special area for cats and kittens," he explained. "If there's one you'd like to hold or play with, I'll get it for you, and you can play with it in the room over there."

She glanced in the direction he was pointing and saw several people sitting on stools, holding cats, and playing with kittens. This was a whole new experience for her.

"Are you a cat lover?" Trent asked.

"I like all animals."

His expression remained soft and pleasant. "Me too, but I have to admit I'm partial to cats." He opened one of the doors on the left and held it for her. As soon as she walked through, she found herself in a maze of large enclosed spaces with cats on one side and kittens on the other. "You've probably noticed that this is kitten season. We've been getting them in faster than we can adopt them out."

"Hey, Trent! We need you up front for a sec."

Trent nodded. "Look around for a little while. I'll be back to help you with whichever kittens you'd like to see."

As Melissa meandered down the long aisle between the cats and kittens, she tried to imagine any of them being hers. The idea of getting an adult cat appealed to her because they were clearly more docile and probably wouldn't get into as much as the curious kittens would.

She stopped and watched a couple of the kittens playing with each other's tails. They were cute and hilarious, but there were so many she couldn't decide which ones she'd like to hold.

"It's hard, isn't it?"

She spun around at the sound of the man's voice behind her. "Daddy, that's Miss Hewitt."

He nodded and extended his hand. "I'm Brandon Woodall, and Olivia told me I had to come back here and meet you."

Now that Melissa knew the little girl's name, she recognized her as being the most advanced student in Elaine's class. In fact, Elaine told her she'd tried to get her moved up to first grade, but her dad didn't like the idea of taking her away from her friends. Olivia's mother had died when Olivia was still a baby, so Elaine said she suspected her dad spent all his free time with her, teaching her things most people left to the teachers.

"I'm Melissa."

"So you're here for a cat, huh?"

Melissa nodded. "It's just so hard to decide which

one."

"Daddy, I like the cute little kittens over there."

Melissa glanced over in the direction where Olivia pointed, toward a couple of kittens perched in a basket. They were so adorable they didn't look real.

"Both of them are so cute." Melissa looked down at Olivia. "Which one do you like?"

"The one that's yellow all over is super cute, but I think I like the one with some white on it better."

Almost as if they could tell they were being discussed, the kittens turned their sweet little faces toward them. Melissa's heart melted. Now she knew which ones she wanted to hold.

Olivia's dad rubbed the back of his neck as a look of regret passed over his face. "I'm afraid it was a huge mistake bringing Olivia back here."

"Daddy, can I please have one of those kittens? I want one *so* bad." The way she dragged out the word "so" almost made Melissa laugh, but she caught herself. However, Brandon didn't hold back.

"Olivia, I've already told you that until you're old enough to do everything for the kitten, we're not getting one."

"I can feed it." Olivia lowered her head and started to pout, but when she glanced up at Melissa, it was obvious she was trying to play her dad.

Melissa decided to do the adult thing and help Brandon out. "There's a lot more to taking care of a pet than feeding it. First of all, there's a litter pan that has to be emptied …"

"Ew." Olivia pinched her nostrils. "That's just gross."

Brandon winked at Melissa before chiming in. "And we have to take it to the vet for shots."

"Poor kitty." Olivia frowned. "I bet that'll make it cry."

"There are so many things you have to do for a cat," Melissa continued.

Olivia tapped her chin with her index finger as she thought about it. "Then why are you getting one?"

Printed in Great Britain
by Amazon